The best summer job ever

Brian was on his feet now.

He saw Davey Schofield grinning at him from the other end of the dugout.

Davey motioned to Brian, letting him know that it was all right for him to join the celebration on the field.

"You wear the uniform, you're part of the team now," Davey said, putting an arm around Brian's shoulders.

Brian walked that way with the Tigers' manager toward home plate, picking up Curtis Keller's bat when he got there. Doing his job.

As far as he was concerned, the best summer job ever invented by mortal minds.

Batboy for the Detroit Tigers.

He was part of the team now.

BOOKS BY MIKE LUPICA

Travel Team

Heat

Miracle on 49th Street

Summer Ball

The Big Field

Million-Dollar Throw

The Batboy

Hero

The Underdogs

True Legend

THE COMEBACK KIDS SERIES:

Hot Hand

Two-Minute Drill

Long Shot

Safe at Home

Shoot-Out

THE
BATBOY

MIKE LUPICA

THE
BATBOY

PUFFIN BOOKS
An Imprint of Penguin Group (USA) Inc.

PUFFIN BOOKS
Published by the Penguin Group
Penguin Young Readers Group, 345 Hudson Street, New York, New York 10014, U.S.A.
Penguin Group (Canada), 90 Eglinton Avenue East, Suite 700, Toronto, Ontario, Canada M4P 2Y3
(a division of Pearson Penguin Canada Inc.)
Penguin Books Ltd, 80 Strand, London WC2R 0RL, England
Penguin Ireland, 25 St Stephen's Green, Dublin 2, Ireland (a division of Penguin Books Ltd)
Penguin Group (Australia), 250 Camberwell Road, Camberwell, Victoria 3124, Australia
(a division of Pearson Australia Group Pty Ltd)
Penguin Books India Pvt Ltd, 11 Community Centre, Panchsheel Park, New Delhi - 110 017, India
Penguin Group (NZ), 67 Apollo Drive, Rosedale, Auckland 0632, New Zealand
(a division of Pearson New Zealand Ltd)
Penguin Books (South Africa) (Pty) Ltd, 24 Sturdee Avenue,
Rosebank, Johannesburg 2196, South Africa

Penguin Books Ltd, Registered Offices: 80 Strand, London WC2R 0RL, England

First published in the United States of America by Philomel Books,
a division of Penguin Young Readers Group, 2010
Published by Puffin Books, a division of Penguin Young Readers Group, 2011

13 15 17 19 20 18 16 14

THE LIBRARY OF CONGRESS HAS CATALOGED THE PHILOMEL EDITION AS FOLLOWS:
Lupica, Mike. The batboy/ Mike Lupica. p. cm.
Summary: Even though his mother feels baseball ruined her marriage to his father, she allows
fourteen-year-old Brian to become a batboy for the Detroit Tigers, who have just drafted
his favorite player back onto the team.
[1. Baseball—Fiction. 2. Batboys—Fiction. 3. Detroit Tigers (baseball team)—Fiction.
4. Detroit (Mich.)—Fiction. 5. Mothers and sons—Fiction.]
I. Title. PZ7.L97914Bat 2010 [Fic]—dc22 200915067

Puffin Books ISBN 978-0-14-241782-9

Design by Richard Amari
Text set in Apollo

Printed in the United States of America

This book is for my mom and dad, who taught me to dream. And, as always, it is for my wife, Taylor, and my four children, Christopher, Alex, Zach, and Hannah, who prove that dreams come true.

ACKNOWLEDGMENTS

Jim Schmakel, clubhouse manager for the Detroit Tigers: a true gentleman of the game.

And the great Katy Dudley.

And finally, my thanks to Michael Green, who kept saying I needed to tell one of my stories about a batboy. I'm just sayin'.

THE
BATBOY

CHAPTER 1

It was one of those moments when Brian felt as if baseball was close enough for him to reach out and touch. Like his hands were around the handle of a bat. Or like he was on the mound, his fingers making sure the seams of the ball felt just right.

One of those moments when he could close his eyes and imagine he was a big-leaguer himself.

One of those moments, really, when he realized why his dad loved the game the way he did. Loved it too much, according to his mom.

Loved it more than anything or anybody.

Bottom of the ninth inning at Comerica Park, the Tigers

having just scored to tie the game, Willie Vazquez, their short-stop, standing on third and representing the winning run.

One out.

And now came the fun part for Brian Dudley, not just be-cause the Tigers had this kind of shot at a walk-off win, but because Brian got to think right along with Davey Schofield, the Tigers' manager, who was perched on the top step of the dugout near the bat rack, on the home side, the third-base side, of Comerica. This was when baseball felt like the great-est reality show in the world.

Willie, the fastest guy on the team and one of the fastest in the American League, was on third because the Tigers' third baseman, Matt Holmes, had just singled him there, bringing home the tying run with the same swing of the bat.

Curtis Keller, the Tigers' center fielder, was at the plate. Curtis could fly, too. And he had some major pop in his bat for a little guy—a good thing, because now all his team needed was a fly ball deep enough to score Willie to win it.

The scary part? For all of Curtis' talent, and his ability to hit the ball hard from the right side against any kind of pitching, lefty or righty, he struck out a lot.

Willie Vazquez liked to joke that Curtis Keller's strike zone had its own area code. "Sometimes Curtis swings and misses when *I'm* at the plate."

If Curtis were to strike out here, then the Tigers would have two outs, the winning run still on third, a sacrifice fly no longer a possibility. And that would leave things up to Mike Parilli, the Tigers' catcher, who was working on a seriously ugly 0-for-4 day.

So what would Davey do?

Brian knew all the stats on Curtis, inside and out, the way he knew the stats on all the Tigers players. Not because anybody had made him learn them. Not because it was some kind of course at school. Brian knew stats because he wanted to know. Because his head was full of the numbers of baseball, all the numbers that not only held the sport together, but connected one season to another, one era to another. Kenny Griffin, Brian's best bud, liked to say that if you could ever crack Brian's head open like a walnut, decimal points would come spilling out.

Now, sitting here at Comerica, feeling like he had the best seat in the house, Brian tried to put those numbers to use the way he knew Davey Schofield would.

They should squeeze, Brian decided.

All Tigers fans knew how much Davey liked to play "small ball," liked to bunt and move runners and steal bases, especially because this year's Tigers didn't have the kind of home-run power they'd had in the past. The only problem with playing small ball right now—and it was a *big* problem, actually—was that Brian knew that even he was a better bunter than Curtis Keller.

More than two months into the season Curtis still didn't

have a single sacrifice bunt, even though he'd been batting number two in the order pretty much since Opening Day. He'd tried a few times. Six times to be exact, Brian knew, and he'd failed to advance the runner each time. Twice he'd even managed to strike out, which wasn't easy when you were bunting.

Yet Brian was sure the bunt was still the right play, especially against the Indians' big right-handed closer, Rafael Fuentes.

Because the other stat bouncing around inside Brian's head like a pinball was that Curtis had never gotten a hit off Rafael Fuentes, was 0-for-14 lifetime. And Mike Parilli, kneeling there in the on-deck circle? He was 1-for-20 against the guy.

If Curtis didn't get the run home, and get it right now, they were as good as in extra innings already.

"Lay one down," Brian said out loud, almost like he couldn't help himself.

From where he sat he had a perfect view of Davey going through all his signals. Those signals went to the Tigers' third-base coach, Nate Vinton, who then flashed them to Curtis. Willie didn't need the middleman; he was staring into the dugout at Davey the same as Nate was. More baseball stuff that Brian loved, the play having this kind of drama even before Rafael Fuentes delivered the ball to the plate.

Brian was never bored by any of it, whether he was at the

ballpark or watching on television. He realized he wasn't just thinking along with Davey, he was thinking along with the Indians' manager at the same time as he brought his corner infielders in and left his shortstop and second base-man in their regular spots, knowing a ground-ball double play would get them out of the inning, provided they could double up a speed guy like Curtis.

It was the first midweek afternoon game since school had let out, and for Brian, this felt like the real start of summer, no matter what the calendar said. Summer was something you could hear and feel all around you at Comerica, filled with all this noise and all these possibilities and all this base-ball. Yeah, this was summer.

Curtis got into the batter's box. Rafael Fuentes was ready to pitch. This close to the field, Fuentes, at 6 foot 4 and 245 pounds, looked as big to Brian as Shaquille O'Neal. Fuentes liked to pitch from the stretch and was doing so now, eye-balling Willie Vazquez as he juked around off third base. One more drama, Brian knew, this one between pitcher and base runner.

Fuentes stood there so long, as if frozen, that Curtis stepped out of the batter's box and went through his whole routine of getting ready again—loosening and refastening his batting gloves, then taking a practice swing.

Brian knew that some people hated all the starts and stops of baseball, all the breaks in the action. Not Brian Dudley. He wasn't ever going to be somebody who came to the ballpark and as soon as he got there acted as if he had somewhere else to be.

When he was at the ballpark, Brian was always where he wanted to be. Sometimes he felt more at home at Comerica than he did at his own home.

Curtis dug back in. Fuentes began his pitching motion, checked quickly one more time on Willie, then blew strike one right past Curtis, high heat, pure cheese, Curtis swinging right through it. The pitch measured 97 mph on the huge scoreboard towering over left field at Comerica.

Lay one down, Brian thought again.

The first and third basemen were still in at the corners, had to be, just to make sure. But they had seen Curtis swing from his heels the way everybody in the ballpark had, like he was trying to hit one all the way to Canada.

Fuentes' right arm came forward again. Another fastball. But Curtis Keller had dropped the head of the bat.

Bunt.

Not the kind of bunt they taught you in Little League, where you squared for a straight sacrifice and practically made an announcement to the infielders that you were bunting. No, this was the way you bunted, even with the third baseman charging in, when you were bunting for a base hit, when you deadened the ball and came racing out of the batter's box like a sprinter in track coming out of the blocks.

Curtis actually laid down a beauty, the ball dying like a toy car that had run out of batteries as Willie Vazquez, coming the other way, blew right past it.

Gus Howell, the Indians' third baseman, made a great play on the ball, flung it sidearm, nearly underhanded, toward home plate. If the runner had been a slow one, the throw might have had a chance. But it was Willie who slid across home plate with the winning run and then bounced right up, clapping his hands, yelling, *"Yeah! Yeah, baby!"*

You had to be close to the field to hear him because all around, from every corner of the ballpark, came the happy roar of Comerica, the sound baseball made when your team won.

The Indians were already walking off the field. Game over. The Tigers in the dugout were pouring out onto the field. Even though it was only June, everybody already knew it was going to come down to the Tigers and the Indians in the American League Central this year. The Tigers had just swept the first series of the season between the two teams—their biggest wins of the young season.

Brian was on his feet now.

He saw Davey Schofield grinning at him from the other end of the dugout.

"Lay one down?" Davey said.

Brian said, "You heard?"

Davey said, "Man, I think the *peanut vendors* heard. Now

I even got a *kid* knowing all my brilliant moves before I make 'em. Must be because your father played."

"Must be," Brian said, the sense of celebration suddenly leaving.

"Where's he now?"

"Japan," Brian said.

Davey motioned to Brian, letting him know that it was all right for him to join the celebration on the field.

"You wear the uniform, you're part of the team now," Davey said, putting an arm around Brian's shoulders.

Brian walked that way with the Tigers' manager toward home plate, picking up Curtis Keller's bat when he got there. Doing his job.

As far as he was concerned, the best summer job ever invented by mortal minds.

Batboy for the Detroit Tigers.

He was part of the team now.

CHAPTER 2

He still couldn't believe he'd gotten the job, over all the other kids in the Detroit area who wanted to spend their summer getting paid to be at Comerica for Tigers home games.

Now that he'd been doing it for a week, Brian realized he'd never really understood as a fan what the job meant. The hours you had to put in every day—eight usually and sometimes nine. All the work you had to do in Equipment Room No. 3 next to the Tigers' dugout before you ever got near the field. Before you could even wear your uniform with "Batboy" on the back instead of a number.

He'd always just assumed that being a batboy meant

collecting foul balls and handing players new bats if they broke one.

He never knew how many pine tar rags were required for every game, how many rosin bags. He didn't know that the Tigers actually employed four batboys: one for the Tigers' dugout and clubhouse, one for the visitors' side, one each to sit down near the stands behind first and third base to collect foul balls.

Brian Dudley, rookie batboy, didn't know that one of his most important jobs once the game was over would be shining shoes for the next game.

He was the son of a pitcher, one who'd survived fourteen seasons pitching in the big leagues, and yet he didn't have a clue what batboys actually did.

And wouldn't have cared a lick if he had.

The way he didn't care that he was being paid $7.50 an hour.

Because the truth was, Brian would have paid them to have this job, if he'd had the money, paid *them* to be on the inside of what had once been his father's world.

Pretty much his father's *whole* world.

It was as if he'd climbed down out of the stands and into a dream, climbed down from where he used to sit with his dad for Tigers games before his dad had walked out on him and his mom for good.

At fourteen, Brian was a decent enough ballplayer, good enough to be the last kid picked for All-Stars this summer from Bloomfield Hills, where he and his mom lived. He was a righty hitter who could hit to all fields, using the whole ballpark the way his dad had taught him, even if he still hadn't hit a home run at any level he'd ever played. And he'd made himself into a solid outfielder even if what he really wanted to be was an infielder. Third base was his spot—the position his man Hank Bishop had played when Brian was old enough to first fall in love with the Detroit Tigers.

But Brian was a realist. He knew he was never going to be an actual big-leaguer himself, and would probably be lucky to make the varsity in high school when the time came.

So this summer was going to be his summer to be a big-leaguer, to be on the inside. Be a Tiger.

It all happened because of a letter he wrote.

Two, actually.

He'd written the first one the summer he'd finished sixth grade. It was the summer his dad left them, even though it felt like his dad had been leaving them for a long time. Until then, baseball and the Tigers had been about the only thing he'd been able to share with Cole Dudley, who'd been one of those specialty left-handed relievers who seem to be able to find work in the big leagues until they finally had run out of arm or run out of stuff. Cole Dudley had pitched for ten different teams in ten different cities in his fourteen years before finally retiring—"about five minutes before baseball retired me"—when he was forty, after one last half season with the Seattle Mariners.

He wasn't bitter about his career ending, or about never having been a star. It was simply that he loved the game too much, and when he tried to live a life without it, with Brian and his mom in the house in Bloomfield, he just couldn't do it.

Brian was eight when his dad retired, and as sad as his dad was about it, Brian was happy, because he would have Cole around all the time then, or so he'd thought.

And for a while, it *was* great for Brian, because baseball was finally something he could share with his dad in *person*. His dad bought them two season tickets up behind the Tigers' dugout on the third-base side with amazing views. Yet for his dad, the seats never seemed close enough. He always looked uncomfortable being so near to the field yet not being *on* it. The game was all he'd known since he was a boy Brian's age.

Even now, Brian could remember the nights when it seemed like he could call every pitch the pitchers were going to throw.

He didn't know how to be a dad with anything else, didn't know how to *talk* to Brian about anything else. But he could talk about baseball and talk about pitching, and when he was gone, it was as if those nights at the ballpark were all he left behind.

That and the note he left on Brian's desk, the one he found when he got home from school one day.

"B—I'm sorry. I'm no good at being your father. I'm no good at anything besides baseball. Dad"

That was the summer Cole Dudley took his first job as a pitching coach, traveling the West Coast as a roving minor-league instructor for the Diamondbacks. He didn't even bother to file for divorce. Brian's mom would do that later.

The very next day Brian went on his computer and found out the name of the Tigers' clubhouse and equipment manager, Jim Schenkel, and wrote him a letter applying for the job of Tigers' batboy.

A few days later he received a letter back from Mr. Schenkel, on Detroit Tigers stationery, telling him that he appreciated the interest, but that twelve-year-old boys were too young to work for the Tigers, and that Brian should get back in touch in a few years. And in the meantime, Mr. Schenkel wrote, Brian had better keep up with his schoolwork, because the big thing he looked for in his batboys was A's.

"And I don't mean the Oakland A's," was the way the letter ended.

Brian didn't tell him that he was Cole Dudley's son, because that summer he didn't feel much like Cole Dudley's son.

That was two summers ago.

Brian knew by now that most batboys in Major League Baseball were sixteen, but he couldn't wait any longer, couldn't bear the idea of having another summer go by and looking out on the field and seeing other kids doing his dream job.

So in April he had written Mr. Schenkel another letter, not a handwritten note this time, typing it out on his computer, his mom making sure the form was exactly right.

The way Brian made sure the words were exactly right.

Dear Mr. Schenkel:

My name is Brian Dudley. Maybe you remember me. I live in Bloomfield Hills with my mom and I wrote you a letter the year before last applying for the job of batboy. You were kind enough to write me back the same week and inform me that I was too young and to get back to you when I was older.

I didn't mention this to you the first time I wrote you, but my dad is Cole Dudley, who was in the major leagues with a lot of teams, even though the Tigers was never one of them.

You also told me to keep my grades up, which I have.

Over the past two years I've worked harder than ever at my schoolwork, telling myself that with every paper I wrote and every test I aced, I was working my way toward Comerica.

I know I'm "officially" too young for the job. But I'm ready for this, Mr. Schenkel. I'm sure every boy who writes you tells you how much they love the Tigers and love baseball. But no one loves the Tigers, or knows them better, than I do. It's not just statistics, it's the history of the team, too. I know that Mayo Smith was the manager when the Tigers came from three-games-to-one down to beat the Cardinals in the 1968 World Series. I know it was Sparky Anderson who said, "Bless you, boys" to the '84 Tigers. I know about Al Kaline and Kirk Gibson and my personal all-time favorite player, Hank Bishop.

Before my dad left my mom and me, he used to take me to Comerica a lot and tell me about when he first started going to Tiger Stadium when he was my age. And even after he left, and I felt like I'd lost a big part of my life, I still had the Tigers.

Maybe there's no way around me being only fourteen. But I hope there is. Working for the Tigers, even if it's just for one summer, is my dream. And my mom, even though she isn't too big on baseball since my dad left, is always telling me that you can't know if your dreams are out of reach until you actually reach for them.

I guess that's what I'm doing with this letter.

Sincerely,
Brian Dudley

When he didn't hear back right away, the way he had the first time he'd applied, he just assumed that he was too young and that was that, end of story.

Ten days later, though, the letter came telling him he had the job.

Mr. Schenkel told him he'd made a copy of Brian's letter and sent it to the commissioner of baseball, Mr. Bud Selig, and that Mr. Selig had called the day he received it and said, "We need more kids like this in baseball, not less, whatever their age is. Whether their dads played in the big leagues or not."

Then, according to Mr. Schenkel, the commissioner of baseball had said to him, "This boy is the boy we all were once."

At the end of the letter Mr. Schenkel asked for Brian's mom to get his school transcript, and explained how she could go online for the rest of the forms she needed to fill out.

At the very end, Mr. Schenkel wrote, "See you when school's out in June, batboy."

His mom didn't like it at first. She talked about what a hassle it would be getting him back and forth from the ballpark, and how it was going to mean rearranging her work schedule—*if* she could even do that. Yet Brian knew it wasn't the hassle that was bothering her, it was that he was getting a job around a Major League Baseball team.

She had thought her life had stopped revolving around baseball a long time ago, and now Brian wanted, more than anything, to go spend a summer working at Comerica Park for the Tigers.

They went around and around on this one night at the dinner table until finally he had said, "Mom, this is my dream."

And she had looked at him hard and said, "Couldn't it be a dream about something else?"

He'd shaken his head.

She'd sighed heavily then, rubbing her temples with her fingers and closing her eyes. Finally, after the longest moment of Brian's life, she said, "Then go for it."

He had the job. And after what felt like about 400 years, especially once the Tigers' season started in April, school had finally ended and summer had arrived.

Now every day and night when there was a home game—and when Brian didn't have a game with All-Stars—his mom would drop him off on Montcalm Street on her way to her job as producer and news writer at WWJ, Detroit's all-news radio station. Brian would walk underneath the pedestrian bridge that connected a parking garage to Comerica, walk through the security entrance to the ballpark, slide his official Tigers' employee card with his picture on it into the time clock—he *never* got tired of doing *that*—and went through the lobby and into the elevator that took him down to the service level.

Once he got down there, Brian would turn left, feeling every time as if he was walking toward the Magic Kingdom of baseball, and travel the thirty or more yards to the Tigers' clubhouse entrance. Then he would walk through the double doors, poke his head into Mr. Schenkel's office on the right to see if he was there, to let him know that he'd arrived for work.

This was usually around three thirty in the afternoon.

After that he'd walk down the steps to the field level. And before he'd go into Equipment Room No. 3 to change his clothes, he'd go into the dugout and walk up the steps and stand on the edge of the green grass of Comerica Park.

And each time, it was as if he was seeing all that green for the first time. Seeing how perfect the infield dirt looked after it had just been raked, and the dirt around the pitcher's mound, and around home plate.

He'd look at the signs in the outfield and the skyline of the city and up to where the announcers' booths were, look around at all the empty seats as if this were the first day that baseball was ever going to be played.

And every day he would go and stand right in front of the Tigers' dugout and count the rows back to the twentieth row where he and his dad used to sit.

Sometimes he would close his eyes and imagine the two of them sitting there, see himself at nine or ten eating popcorn or a hot dog with one hand, his glove on the other.

Brian had the best seat in the house now, he knew that.

But those two seats had once seemed like the best in the world.

CHAPTER 3

They were in Kenny Griffin's backyard, at his house on Yarmouth Road, playing Home Run Derby with a Wiffle ball. Kenny had just taken a break to run into the house and get them a couple of Gatorades.

When he came back outside, he said to Brian, "This just went from being a good day to a great day. Like an instant national sports holiday, practically."

"Why?" Brian said, taking one of the plastic bottles from him. "Did you figure out a way to hit a six-run homer while you were taking so long inside?"

"No, it's not that," Kenny said. "It's because I finally know something about baseball that you don't."

"I would put that down as dubious," Brian said.

It was Saturday afternoon, two days after the Tigers had beaten the Indians in the ninth. Baseball practice was over, but Brian and Kenny weren't baseballed out because they never were. So they were using Home Run Derby, a marathon game, to kill time before the Tigers played the Red Sox at Fenway Park on Fox's *Saturday Game of the Week*.

It was the beginning of a ten-game road trip for the Tigers. Batboys didn't travel with the team, though Brian had heard from Mr. Schenkel that rules like that sometimes had a way of changing if they made the playoffs. But for now Brian's team was in Boston and he was behind Kenny Griffin's house trying to hit balls over the pool fence and into the water.

Already he felt funny, like he'd been cut loose from something now that the Tigers were away, like the circus had up and left town without him.

"Let me get this straight," Brian said, plastic bat in hand. "You're saying you now have a baseball fact that you didn't have before you went inside?"

"Correct."

"A stat?"

"No, Stat Boy. Not one of Brian Dudley's fun facts."

"So are you planning on telling me? Or do I have to beat it out of you with a Wiffle bat?"

"Well," Kenny said, "since you're asking so nicely . . . when I checked my computer, guess what I saw on ESPN.com?"

"Not a clue."

"Only this," Kenny said. "The Detroit Tigers, *our* Detroit Tigers, just added some power to their lineup. Announced in Boston about an hour ago."

Brian could always tell when his best bud was busting his chops and when he was being serious, because he was generally easier to read than a text message.

He was being serious now.

"Tell me," Brian said, "or I *will* beat you."

Kenny, the best pitcher on their team, the Bloomfield Sting, smiled as if he'd just struck out the side.

"Hank Bishop," he said.

"No . . . stinking . . . way," Brian said.

"Way," Kenny said. "Way back, from like the dead, practically."

Hank Bishop had been out of baseball for a year and a half, first because of a fifty-game steroids suspension, then because no club in either league had signed him this spring when he was eligible to play again. He was thirty-five now, about to turn thirty-six on the Fourth of July. Brian knew that the way he knew everything there was to know about Hank Bishop.

But now the Tigers, who needed a right-handed bat to come off the bench and act as a designated hitter occasionally, had brought him back to Detroit, given him one last chance to be something close to what he was.

"This is really happening?" Brian said. "No joke?"

"You think I would joke with *you*?" Kenny said. "About *him*?"

"Excellent point."

"Your boy's back," Kenny said. "Back on the batboy's team."

And wearing the same uniform, Brian thought.

It was all in there, everything that Brian already knew about the way Hank Bishop's career had started out, and the way it had ended, with him ten home runs short of the magic number of 500.

Only the Tigers had changed all that in Boston.

"We're not asking him to be what he was," Davey Schofield was quoted as saying. "But from what I saw in batting practice this morning, there's a place for him on this baseball team."

If Hank Bishop hadn't been the best player in baseball by the time he'd been in the big leagues three seasons, he was, as Brian's dad liked to say, in the conversation.

He was MVP in the American League the year he turned twenty-five, still playing shortstop that year. From then until he turned thirty, he hit between thirty-five and forty-five home runs every season, knocked in at least a hundred, and scored at least a hundred. He kept hitting even after his first knee operation, and there wasn't a baseball fan in Detroit or anywhere else who wasn't sure he was on his way to the Hall of Fame.

The sportswriters in Detroit started out calling him the Bishop of Baseball in Detroit. That was long before the first real trouble he got into, when he got arrested for a fight outside a bar and spent the night in jail and one of the papers ran the headline "Hank in the Tank."

But there was much worse trouble to come, only nobody knew it at the time and everybody was willing to forgive him—starting with Brian—because he just kept hitting.

"The only way they stop forgiving you in sports," Brian's dad once said, "is when you stop producing."

Hank kept producing. Even after that arrest, even after the first knee operation, even after his move over to third base. The Tigers weren't making the playoffs in those years, and so there were seasons when he was the best reason to keep watching, or keep going to the ballpark.

But then the trouble began multiplying. It wasn't just a fight in a bar. Hank Bishop seemed to fight with everybody—his teammates and his manager and sportswriters and talk show hosts, and finally there were two straight years when he didn't get to thirty home runs and didn't come close to knocking in a hundred and that was it as far as Detroit was concerned. The Tigers traded him away to the Angels. That was when he had his first positive test for steroids and got suspended, even though he blamed it on some shot he said he'd gotten from one of his teammates.

He ended up in the National League after that, with the Rockies, and then came his second positive test, the one that got him suspended for fifty games, the rules tougher by then. He served it out last season and then wasn't even offered an invitation to spring training. That's when Brian realized just how right his dad had been. Now that Hank Bishop couldn't hit the ball out of sight anymore, everyone had stopped forgiving him. In the minds of most baseball fans, Hank Bishop had committed the two worst possible sins:

Not only had he used steroids, he'd gotten *caught* using them.

Brian had never wanted to forgive him on either count, because he loved baseball too much not to see what guys using those drugs had done to the records and the record books in his lifetime. But he couldn't help it: He never stopped rooting for Hank Bishop, even when he was off playing for other teams, and he knew why:

Hank was the first guy in sports who made him want to watch and, even more important than that, he was the first guy to make him care.

He watched the first five innings of the game at Kenny's, by which time the Tigers were ahead 6–0 behind their best starter, Ben Dillon. But that didn't mean Brian was going to put this one in the books or stop watching, because this was still Fenway Park, where bad things could happen to big leads. It was something Brian had always loved about baseball, that you couldn't run out the clock, that you had to find a way to get twenty-seven outs.

Kenny asked if he wanted to stay for dinner and then sleep over, since sleepovers were usually the rule on weekends, either here or at Brian's house. But Brian's mom had made a point of asking him to be home for dinner tonight, just the two of them, and Brian was pretty sure he knew why:

This was the sixteenth wedding anniversary for her and his dad, even though his dad was long gone.

Brian wasn't sure why this date was one more stat he knew, but he did.

He didn't explain why he couldn't stay, just told Kenny his mom had planned a special dinner and that he was going to bounce.

"If I leave now, I can be home by the time we finish batting in the top of the sixth," Brian said.

"Boy, that's a big load off," Kenny said. "I don't think Dillon could get through the heart of the order without you watching."

"You still don't believe I can directly influence the outcome of these games, do you?" Brian said.

"As long as you believe, Bri, bro, that's all that matters."

"I bet they get Hank right in there tomorrow," Brian said. "He always had huge numbers at Fenway, and the Sox have a lefty going."

"Can I ask you something before you go?" Kenny said. "I get why Bishop *was* your guy when he was with the Tigers the first time. But how can he still be now? You know, like after everything that's happened since he left?"

It was hard to understand, Brian knew that. And if he even tried to explain it now, he wasn't going to make it home by the time the Red Sox came to bat in the bottom of the sixth at Fenway.

So he just tossed a line at his friend over his shoulder as he headed off to get his bike, gave him enough of an honest answer to get him by.

"At least Hank came back," Brian said.

CHAPTER 4

Liz Dudley had no use for baseball. She went to as many of Brian's games as she could, and he knew how much she wanted him to do well. Yet he knew she wanted to be somewhere else—*anywhere* else—except a ballgame.

Baseball to his mom was like some foreign language she'd had to learn in school and then never wanted to use again.

She had met her future husband at a charity dinner in Detroit the first winter after she'd graduated from the University of Michigan. He was thirty and had already been in the majors for five years, and she was twenty-two, interning at the ESPN radio station in Detroit—not because she was a sports fan, but just because she wanted to get into radio. A friend who actually was a baseball fan introduced them, and they got married a year later.

A year after that Brian was born.

Cole Dudley never lasted more than a season or two with one team. And Liz Dudley finally announced she wasn't going to tour the American and National Leagues anymore, not with a baby. She moved back to the Detroit area, first to her hometown of Perrysburg, Ohio, about an hour away from Detroit, and then to Bloomfield Hills after she got her current radio job.

By the time Brian was old enough to go to school, the only time he saw his dad was between the end of the season in October and the beginning of spring training for pitchers and catchers in February.

"For most of our marriage," Brian's mom said to him one time, "I looked at baseball as the other woman."

"You know what I really felt when he finally left?" she'd said that day. "Relieved. Because I didn't have to compete with baseball anymore."

So now it was just the two of them, the table set permanently for two, Brian and his mom having dinner together on the unmentioned anniversary, his dad not calling her today because he never called her. He was in Japan now working as a pitching coach. Neither one of them had heard from him in months, not even on Brian's birthday. The dad he knew was never coming back.

Sometimes Brian wondered if his dad still loved baseball as much, even on the other side of the world. More often, he wondered if his dad ever missed him.

His mom had come up big tonight with dinner, made him all his favorite stuff: cheeseburgers on the grill, fried onions to go on top, homemade french fries, even mashed potatoes, maybe his favorite dish in the whole world, on the side. She had timed it out perfectly, too, putting the food out about five minutes after the end of the game, the Tigers having hung on for a 6–4 victory, closer Brad Morley pitching them out of a bases-loaded jam in the bottom of the ninth.

"I can't believe you doubled down with mashed potatoes on top of the fries," Brian said.

"Think of it as a hearty postgame meal," she said. "Even with the postgame buffet in the clubhouse, your father used to come home and eat like he'd just ended some kind of fast."

They didn't talk much about him anymore. He wondered why she did so now. Maybe it was because of the anniversary.

He smothered the fries in some hot sauce, saw his mom wince as he did. "Don't worry," he said. "I'm just trying to put a little hair on my chest."

"Better you than me," she said. "I used to wait for your father to pour hot sauce on his breakfast cereal."

Brian didn't know how he was supposed to respond to

that, never knew if his mom even *wanted* a response when the subject of his dad came up, so he did what he did a lot.

Changed the subject.

"I still can't believe we got Hank Bishop back!"

"He's pretty old now, isn't he?" his mom said.

Brian said, "Not really. In fact, he's not even as old as . . ."

He knew he had stopped himself too late.

"As old as your sainted mother?" Liz Dudley said.

"You know, that just came out flat wrong," Brian said. "The two of you are practically the same age. He turns thirty-six later this summer." He grinned at her, sighed, and then said, "Moving right along."

Now they both laughed.

"Let me ask you something, though," his mom said. "Weren't we still hating on him not long ago because of the whole steroids thing?"

"Sort of," he said. "He was totally stupid, no doubt. Twice stupid, as a matter of fact. But he's cleaned up his act now."

"And we know he's cleaned up . . . because?"

"Because," Brian said, "the Tigers wouldn't have signed him if he hadn't. And because if he ever tests positive again, he'll be banned from baseball for life."

She smiled now, mostly to herself, and said, "That's what I keep trying to be. Banned from baseball for life."

Brian leaned forward, hands out, almost like he was reaching for her. "Mom," he said, "you get why this is a totally cool thing, right? What a cool thing this can be for Hank and the Tigers? Because if he has a good season, then all the drug stuff and the way he's messed up won't be the last thing people remember about him. This is a way for him to get people to remember how great he used to be."

"The way you do," she said.

"Well, maybe not *exactly* the way I do," he said. "I just don't want him to go out with the whole world still hating on him for steroids."

She nodded and said, "Honey, if you're happy, then I'm happy."

Brian knew she wanted to mean it.

"So how did practice go today?" she asked.

Brian reminded her about how his first games with his travel team would be played at home next weekend.

And then it was quiet at the table, the way it often was when his mom finally ran out of the questions she felt she was supposed to ask about baseball. When they both ran out of things to say to each other. It was happening more and more, them having so little to say to each other when the subject wasn't baseball that Brian wondered if it used to be the exact same way when she and his dad sat at this same table.

When he got up to his room, Brian went into his closet and got out the box labeled "Hank Bishop."

It was all in there. The issue of *Sports Illustrated* with Hank on the cover from the summer when Brian was eight. The autographed ball that his mom had bought for him at a Field of Dreams store in Indianapolis when she'd been at a radio convention there last summer, the one that Brian had taken off his desk and put in the box with the rest of the Hank stuff when he'd gotten suspended for drugs the first time. There was the autographed picture the Tigers' public relations department had sent to him, one that read, "To a future Tiger! All the best! Hank Bishop."

Then there were the game programs, from every game Brian had ever seen Hank Bishop play in person. There was the shoe box inside the bigger box with all of his Hank Bishop baseball cards. His first glove, too small for him now, a Hank Bishop model TPX.

And at the very bottom of the box, in a manila envelope, were the Comerica ticket stubs.

Brian went through them now and found the stub from the very first game he'd watched Hank play, eight years ago against the Yankees, on July 27, the first time he'd ever seen a big-league game in person. Hank Bishop had hit two home runs that night, the last a walk-off job to win the game in the bottom of the thirteenth.

And, all this time later, Hank Bishop was back. He really *had* come back into Brian's world. And he knew, even in his great baseball heart, that he shouldn't be this stoked about it, as stoked as he'd sounded at dinner with his mom. But he was. He just was. He remembered how hurt he'd been when he'd found out Hank Bishop—his guy—had been enough of a dope to start using dope.

Not hurt the way he had been when his dad left. But hurt by sports in a way that Brian never thought it could.

Now the fan in him couldn't wait for the Tigers' road trip to end, couldn't wait for them to get back to Comerica, couldn't wait to be in the same dugout with Hank Bishop, in the same clubhouse. The same field.

He wished he could have explained it better to his mom at dinner—why this was so important to him. He wished he could have made her understand. She had tried, the way she always tried, in those moments when he knew she was trying to be both mother and father to him at the same time. She just didn't get it. And Brian understood that, he really did. She couldn't be everything to him, and he wasn't going to love her any less because she didn't love baseball the way he did.

But sometimes he couldn't help himself, no matter how hard he tried, no matter how dumb he told himself he was being, no matter how mad it made him to open the door even a crack.

Sometimes he missed his dad.

CHAPTER 5

During the regular season, Brian and Kenny had played in the thirteen–fourteen division of Bloomfield Little League. Now they were with the Sting, playing in a travel league called the North Oakland Baseball Federation. The winner of their league would head to the state tournament, which this year would be played about twenty minutes away, at Liberty Park in Sterling Heights, at the end of August.

Sometimes they'd play a three-game weekend series against the same team, either the Motor City Hit Dogs or Clarkson River Rebels or Lake Orion Dragons. Sometimes they'd play in Bloomfield, occasionally in Birmingham, going over to Memorial Park in Royal Oak for a night game, because Memorial had lights. Before the regular season was over, they'd have played thirty games.

Brian had already gotten his batboy job when it came time to try out for travel ball, and before he did, he told Coach Joe Johnson that even if he made the team, he would have to miss some games because of his job. But when Coach Johnson heard what the job was, he smiled.

"I was a batboy with the White Sox the summer I turned sixteen," he said. "Best summer of my whole life."

Then Coach Johnson had said he'd check with the board of directors for Bloomfield Little League about adding an extra player this summer, giving one more kid a chance to play with the Sting.

"Nothing a coach likes better than a win-win situation," Coach said. "I feel like I just won a doubleheader."

Brian checked with Mr. Schenkel, who said that a lot of his batboys played on travel teams and tournament teams in the summer, and that he was sure he could get together with Coach Johnson to come up with a schedule that would work for everybody, especially since Brian wouldn't be traveling with the Tigers.

When Coach Johnson got the preliminary schedule for the Sting, he e-mailed it to Brian's mom, who e-mailed it to Mr. Schenkel. By the end of that week they had all come up with a way for him to play the five weekends when the Tigers were on the road during the Sting's season and get enough time off from the Tigers when the Tigers were at home to play at least twenty of the Sting's thirty games.

Brian told Mr. Schenkel that he wanted to miss as few Tigers games as possible, that as much as he loved playing travel ball with his friends, his job was his first priority. He just wanted to make sure that Mr. Schenkel understood that he'd spend every day and night of the summer at Comerica if he could.

The first series of the season for the Sting was against one of the two teams from Rochester, the Rockies, who had made the state finals the year before. But Kenny had shut them out on Friday night, and now the Sting seemed to be on their way to an easy win at the West Hills field on Saturday afternoon.

It was 5–0 after three innings, but that was when things started to fall apart behind Brendan DePonte, their number-two starter. And the trouble actually started because of their number-one starter, Kenny Griffin, who played shortstop when he wasn't pitching.

With two outs in the top of the fourth, bases loaded, the score still 5–0, the Rochester cleanup batter hit what looked like the dream double-play ball of all time right at Kenny, who wasn't just the best arm the Sting had, but the best pure hitter and the best fielder. Sometimes Brian thought Kenny had even better hands than Willie Vazquez, the Tigers' shortstop.

Not this time.

Kenny came up and out of the ball way too soon, as if he

could already see himself flipping the ball to Kyle Nichols, coming over to second. So instead of his fielding the ball cleanly, it bounced off the heel of Kenny's glove, rolling to his left. Then, when he hurried to pick up the ball, he managed to kick it into short center instead. By then the score was 5–2, runners on second and third for the Rockies.

The inning turned into a nightmare after that, as Brendan completely lost his composure. The Rockies got four more hits and scored five more runs, and by the time the Sting got back to the dugout, they were losing, 7–5. Different day, different game. It was one of the beauties of sports, how fast things changed.

Except you didn't think it was so beautiful when it happened to you, especially after ringing up the kind of lead they'd had against one of the best teams they were going to see all summer.

Kyle hit a home run in the bottom of the seventh to get them back to 7–6, but that was the way it stayed until the bottom of the ninth. Brian was batting seventh tonight and had gone 1-for-3. He'd doubled down the left-field line in the second, knocking in a run and then coming around to score himself. He'd lined out twice after that, and walked right after Matt's home run in the seventh, never moving off first.

And now, with the Sting up to bat for last licks, the lineup had worked itself around to him.

Kenny had walked with two outs. Then Andrew Clark, their catcher, managed to squeeze a ground-ball single between the first and second basemen. The Rockies' right fielder charged the ball like a champ, holding Kenny to second. But still:

Tying run on second, winning run on first, game on Brian's bat if he could hit one hard someplace.

Game on *him*, in the first big weekend of travel ball.

He didn't expect it to happen this way very often. Brian knew he wasn't one of the real stars on this team, and he almost wished it was Kenny or Kyle who had this chance to win the game. They were the ones who were supposed to be up with the game on the line.

Yet it was Brian up at bat. Against the Rockies' closer, the biggest kid in the game, a real load, but one who could throw just as hard as Kenny could.

He dug in and locked eyes on Kenny's as Kenny took his short lead off second. And Kenny must have been thinking right along with him, because he pointed at Brian now with the index fingers of both hands and mouthed these words as he did:

Be the man.

Brian nodded, got himself set, and then proceeded to swing right through strike one. Stepped out, rubbed some dirt on his hands, took a deep breath, stepped back in, set his bat.

And looked even worse swinging through strike two.

The man? Brian felt like a little boy. But then he caught a break. The Rockies' closer tried way too hard to strike him out on the next two pitches, like he was Brad Morley of the Tigers trying to amp up the radar gun to 100 mph. He missed wild and high both times. Only a great reach by the Rockies' catcher on the second one kept Kenny from advancing to third.

There were no stats for Brian to fall back on now, no matchup numbers. All those decimal points inside his head were totally useless. The only numbers that mattered were these: 2–2. The only thing that mattered was finding a way to do something all hitters tried to do in moments like this:

Figure out a way to catch up with the other guy's fastball.

Brian guessed that the next pitch would come right down the middle. One of those hit-me-if-you-can pitches.

Brian did.

He kept his head on the ball, made sure not to pull off it, kept his hands back when the impulse was to rush them through.

And when he did bring his hands through, he gave the ball a ride.

For one split second he thought this was finally the one, thought he had hit it hard enough to clear the left-field fence. Not just get a real jack finally, but a walk-off jack at that. But as much of a rope as it was, the ball didn't have the elevation.

What it did have was enough smash to split the left fielder and center fielder and roll all the way to the wall, scoring Andrew with the run that gave the Sting an 8–7 win.

Brian wasn't sure how to act at first.

By the time he got to second, it was as if he'd forgotten all the rules of baseball, which he knew as well as he knew all his numbers. So he put on the brakes and stopped right there, afraid to leave the bag, even after Andrew had crossed.

And it was there, at second base, where Kenny Griffin got his arms around him and his momentum sent them both tumbling onto the outfield grass at West Hills.

Before the rest of the Sting got there, Kenny yelled, "Bro, you know what you are today, right?"

"Get off me, you lunatic," Brian said, enjoying the moment even as Kenny crushed him.

"Bro," Kenny said, "you're the Bishop of Bloomfield!"

Bishop. As in Hank Bishop. It was a name Brian didn't mind one bit.

CHAPTER 6

Brian had come early his first day of work at Comerica, had his mom drop him off at two in the afternoon for a seven o'clock game, and even then he'd seen that manager Davey Schofield was already there, all his coaches were already there, and so were most of the players.

The players didn't have to officially be there until three o'clock, but even that first day Brian could see the looks guys who showed up right on time got.

Like: Where have *you* been?

So from that first day, Brian knew something: Even big-league ballplayers wanted to be here as much as he did.

It was as if they couldn't wait to leave their real homes for their baseball home, to get here and be part of the team—despite all the time they'd already spent together, beginning with spring training.

His mom said it used to be the exact same way for his dad. Once Christmas was over, she said, it was like he kept checking his watch, waiting for it to be time for him to leave for Florida or Arizona.

No matter how late a night game ended, even if it went deep into extra innings, they would be back early the next day, ready to do it again. Another day of the longest season in all of pro sports. It had taken only a couple of weeks, but Brian was beginning to understand what it was like to be a part of this world within a world: the world of the clubhouse, the dugout, the game, of *baseball*.

Some of these players had been only five or six years older than Brian when they'd first gotten to be a part of this world, and it was as if once they did, they never wanted to leave. As if this was a place where they never had to grow up.

The Tigers had returned from their road trip, ready to start a four-game series, all night games, against the Angels. Brian asked his mom if he could show up real early.

Like it was the first day all over again.

"This wouldn't have anything to do with your man Hank coming home today, would it?" his mom said.

"Maybe it does, maybe it doesn't," he said.

Because she was the station's best news writer and one of their senior producers, and because the station was all news all day and night, Brian's mom could pretty much make up her own schedule. And for this summer in her son's life, she had managed to organize it as best she could around the Tigers' schedule. So she was working four to midnight when the Tigers were in town, dropping Brian off on her way to the station. After the game, Brian would get a ride home with Mr. Schenkel, who lived in Bloomfield Village, or with Finn Simpkins, another one of the batboys, who lived a few minutes away from the Dudleys, over near the famous Oakland Hills golf club. And sometimes Liz Dudley would be the one driving Brian and Finn home.

Today she dropped off Brian underneath the walking bridge over Montcalm at a few minutes before two. She never got out of the car, never walked him to the door. Like this was as close to Comerica—to this world—as she wanted to get.

Brian checked himself in, got on the elevator, went down to the service level like always, amazed at how normal this felt to him already—as normal as walking into his own room.

When he walked through the double doors today, he didn't even stop to say hello to Mr. Schenkel, just kept going right into the clubhouse.

And saw that Hank Bishop was already there. Like he had walked right out of one of Brian's baseball cards.

Here he was. Brian really felt like he was in a movie theater, only the star had walked right off the screen and into the audience.

Brian saw that Mr. Schenkel had placed Hank's locker between Willie Vazquez, the life of the team and the life of the clubhouse, and Marty McBain, the team's veteran left fielder and one of the few Tigers left who had been around when Hank Bishop was still playing third and batting third.

Marty had even played with Cole Dudley when both of them were with the Mariners. The team knew by now that Cole Dudley was Brian's father, and every once in a while somebody would ask Brian where his dad was, what he was doing, and he'd tell them.

Brian hadn't noticed Finn hanging back near where the coffeepots were, staring across the room the same as Brian was. But now he heard Finn, in a low voice—batboys were supposed to be seen and not heard—saying, "The man, the legend."

Brian answered in a total whisper. "Oh, baby."

Finn said, "Like he never left."

"He probably wishes that's the way things had worked out," Brian said.

He looked the same, at least to Brian, looked like the guy they'd always said was too big to play shortstop, even though he once played the living daylights out of the position, covering as much ground as anybody in the league at 6 foot 3 and 225 pounds. Maybe he was a little skinnier than that now. And maybe he looked more tired than Brian remembered.

But he was still Hank Bishop.

In the flesh.

There was a home-white No. 24 jersey hanging in his locker. Mr. Schenkel, who handed out numbers to new players if they didn't request a particular number, had never let anybody else wear No. 24 for the Tigers even though the number wasn't officially retired.

So there was his old uniform, looking brand new. Brian wondered if everything felt brand new to Hank Bishop today, as if he'd be starting all over again once he put on his uniform.

He kept staring. So did Finn. Mostly Brian wondered why Hank Bishop, who'd been away from baseball for as long as he had, who'd been given the baseball version of a prison sentence, didn't look happier.

Brian just wanted to stand there and watch for a while, watch the guy's moves with his teammates and with the media when they were allowed in. But both he and Finn knew there was another of Mr. Schenkel's big rules for his batboys:

Once they were at the ballpark, they'd better get busy. And stay busy.

Brian knew by now that usually rookie batboys like himself and Finn started on the visitors' side of Comerica, that working on the Tigers' side was something you had to earn. But all of the batboys were rookies this summer, and so Mr. Schenkel had had to choose, and he had chosen Brian and Finn.

"I always liked watching your dad pitch," he'd said, "because he *knew* how to get outs even when he didn't have his best stuff. And, on top of that, you wrote the best letter this year."

So Brian and Finn went down to Equipment Room No. 3—or simply "No. 3," as they now called it—to change into their pregame uniforms: what looked like a blue Tigers' golf shirt, worn with their uniform pants. They wouldn't put their regular jerseys on until four thirty, when it was time to go out for batting practice.

It was just like any other day.

Only it wasn't.

"You think he can still do it?" Finn said. "At the plate, I mean?"

"I don't think Mr. Schofield would have brought him back if he couldn't," Brian said.

"But if he's not doing steroids anymore . . ." Finn stopped himself. Finn Simpkins had red hair and more freckles than anybody Brian knew, and had just turned sixteen but was small for his age. He played baseball, too, but had told Brian he was nothing more than a scrub on his Juniors team, and hadn't even tried out for tournament ball. Finn didn't know as much baseball history as Brian, but he seemed to love the game just as much. "You think the steroids helped him hit as many home runs as he did?"

Brian blew out some air. "I think they helped everybody," he said. "Hitters, pitchers, everybody who used them. It stinks, just thinking about it, how they screwed up the record books. But it's a fact. And if it's a fact for everybody else, it's a fact for Hank Bishop."

The two boys began going through their list of supplies, even though it was still early. They wanted to make sure that all the work they usually did before batting practice was done so they could be on the field when Hank Bishop took his first cuts.

But it wasn't just that. Brian and Finn knew how things worked with Mr. Schenkel, because it was another thing he'd told them their very first day:

The harder you worked, the more prepared you were, the more likely you were to *stay* on the home team side of Comerica Park this summer, to not have to switch over to the visitors' side, the first-base side, which Finn referred to as "Siberia."

So the two of them went around the room, making sure

everything was in order and fully stocked. Pine tar? Check. Cups? Check. Sunflower seeds—which the players could devour in epic proportions?

Check.

Sugarless gum and Bazooka and Big League Chew?
Check.

The two of them went back to the clubhouse and made sure they didn't have to refill the coffee machine. Mr. Schenkel gave them some shoes that needed shining. Brian and Finn took care of that. When they got back down to No. 3, it was almost time to lug the coolers of Gatorade up to the dugout.

Brian grinned at Finn and said, "I am mad, stupid excited."

"No kidding," Finn Simpkins said. "I hadn't picked up on that."

By four thirty, Brian and Finn had been in their real uniforms for half an hour. So were Matt Connors and Adam Price, the batboys working for the Angels tonight.

It had been unusual for Brian to watch the bottom of the ninth against the Indians from the dugout, Davey Schofield being like most managers and not wanting his batboy running back and forth in front of him and obscuring his vision of the field. But that game had been an exception, Davey seeing how much Brian was into the game, giving him a chance to experience a great bottom of the ninth from inside. Most of the time Brian was in a chair set up on the field, right next to the end of the dugout closest to home plate.

For most of the game that was where he sat, unless he was fetching a bat or running new baseballs to the home-plate umpire. Finn's chair was down the third-base line, at the point where the stands were closest to the field.

Finn had told Brian his name for the summer should be Foul Ball Simpkins.

For now, though, the two of them got to enjoy watching batting practice. Brian still felt stupid excited as he watched Hank Bishop get ready to take his cuts with the rest of the regulars. Davey Schofield would be using him as his DH tonight and batting him fifth in the order.

The Tigers' first-base coach, Rudy Tavarez, was throwing batting practice today. Rudy had been at the end of his career as the Tigers' second baseman when Hank Bishop had first come up with the team. As Hank came around from behind the batting cage now, Rudy yelled, "Oh, man, am I seeing a *ghost*?"

Hank just gave him a little wave. The gates had been opened early today, so there were a lot of fans in the stands, and they gave Hank his first cheer of the day now. It wasn't much, the cheer almost sounding as if it came from outside, but it was enough for him to give a brief tip of his batting helmet.

Hank was ready to hit.

Brian noticed that everything seemed to stop inside Comerica. Even some of the Tigers players warming up in front of the dugout, to Brian's left, had stopped throwing or stretching. The media, so much more media than Brian had seen for batting practice in the first games he had worked, crowded to the front of the rope lines that had been set up in front of both dugouts.

Brian stopped watching them, focused on Hank Bishop. He laced the first pitch he saw over the screen in front of Rudy Tavarez and over Rudy's head, and Brian saw that his batting stance hadn't changed a bit in his time away from the game:

Bat held high and held completely still as he waited for the pitch. No waggling of the bat or extra movement from Hank Bishop. Hardly any stride at all.

He hit one out of the park on his third swing, the ball hit so hard and so high as it came off his maple that for a moment it looked as if it might go crashing into the scoreboard in left, the one Brian felt hovered over Comerica like a satellite.

It didn't. But it cleared the wall with ease. Now there was a bigger batting practice cheer. Hank kept swinging. Nobody had made any announcement around the cage, but it was clear that he was getting extra swings, maybe because everybody just wanted him to get his bearings back.

Or maybe just out of respect.

He ended up hitting two more out, the last one to dead center, which at Comerica could feel like hitting a ball over the moon. When he left the cage, Brian was hoping he might walk over and hand him his bat, the way some of the guys did when they were done with BP. But he didn't. He just walked past Brian and Finn, down the steps, put his bat in with the other ones already in the rack, and placed his batting helmet, looking as new as his uniform did, with the others.

Then he walked down the tunnel toward the clubhouse. Brian watched him go and then said to Finn, "Be right back to help you start cleaning up, swear."

He followed Hank Bishop.

When Brian got to the clubhouse, the only two players in front of their lockers were Hank and Edwin Rosario, tonight's starting pitcher. Edwin was facing into his locker, listening to music on his iPod. Hank Bishop walked across the room, poured himself a cup of black coffee, the coffee that Mr. Schenkel had showed Brian and Finn how to make superstrong for the players, and walked back to his locker.

Brian had learned that Hank's locker used to be on the other side of the clubhouse, in the corner, but that one now belonged to Curtis Keller. Mr. Schenkel had also told Brian that nobody in the big leagues ever gave up a corner locker without a fight.

As soon as Hank Bishop sat down, Brian took a deep breath and walked across the room himself.

When he was standing in front of his idol, he said, "Mr. Bishop, my name is Brian Dudley and I'm one of the new batboys." The words came tumbling out of him, like a spill he'd have to clean up later. "And I just wanted you to know that you've always been my favorite player and not just when you played for the Tigers. And besides that I just wanted you to know how happy I am that you're back with us."

He stuck out his hand. Hank Bishop looked at it, then up at Brian's face, and smiled.

It was the first time Brian had seen him smile all day.

"I'm sorry?" he said.

"I just wanted you to know how happy I am you're back," Brian said.

"I get that," Hank said. "What I don't get is . . . was I talking to anybody?"

"Were you . . . ?" Brian said. Not getting this. "No, sir."

He was looking right at Brian, the smile still in place.

"Then don't talk to me," Hank Bishop said.

CHAPTER 7

Brian stayed away from Hank Bishop the rest of the night and told Finn he probably ought to do the same.

"Maybe he's just freaked about this being his first game back," Finn said. "I'm just putting that out there."

"I'm just putting *this* out there," Brian said. This was a few minutes before the first pitch. "I'm not even making eye contact with the guy from now until we're in the car going home."

And he didn't, not for all nine innings of a game the Tigers finally lost, 4–2. And that wasn't easy with a DH, because they didn't play in the field, which meant they were around twice as much as the guys who were.

Brian had noticed in the past that the Tigers' DHs would often go down to the clubhouse in the top half of an inning. Some guys would watch a replay of their last at-bat on the big flat-screen TV in the players' lounge, where that night's game was always being TiVo-ed. Some would ride the stationary bike to keep themselves warm. When Bobby Moore, the team's regular first baseman, was DH-ing, he'd go down to the batting cage and either hit off a tee or have one of the coaches throw him some extra BP.

Brian would make sure to tell them that if they needed anything, a new T-shirt or jersey or batting gloves, to just let him know. One night Willie Vazquez had DH-ed when he was a little banged up from playing the field. He'd ended up changing jerseys after his first two at-bats.

"Duds, get me some new duds," he'd told Brian. "No hits in what I got on."

Tonight, Brian made absolutely no attempt to follow Hank Bishop around between his at-bats. He just stayed in his chair and did his job. He was still rooting for Hank to get hits, every time up. And he did get one in his second at-bat, a hard single over the shortstop's head that got him a standing ovation from the crowd. And Brian knew he was going to keep rooting for Hank the way he always had.

Even if he was still stinging from what the guy had said to him.

Was I talking to anybody?

With that smile on his face. His magazine-cover smile. Or the TV smile you'd see from him in the old days, after he'd found a way to win the Tigers another game.

Then don't talk to me.

Hank had that same smile on his face when the game was over and he was talking to the media again. There was even a time when Brian was across the locker room and heard a big laugh from the crowd surrounding Hank's locker.

Funny Hank Bishop.

This was one of the nights when it was his mom's turn to drive him and Finn home. As they walked out of the stadium, Brian couldn't help but think how the day had begun a lot better than it had ended. And it had nothing to do with the game.

Brian had waited his whole life to meet Hank Bishop. What felt like his whole life, anyway. For all the pictures he owned, there had been one above all others he'd carried inside his head from the time he'd started rooting for the Tigers and rooting for Hank Bishop:

What it would be like the day he finally shook his hand.

The guy was nicer to his *bat.*

It was a quiet ride home, once Liz Dudley gave up on trying to get any news out of either one of them.

But Brian had to hand it to his old mom, she kept trying.

"So what was he like?" she said.

"I really didn't get to talk to him very much," Brian said.

He was in the backseat with Finn, who added, "I didn't get to talk to him at all."

"But you say you did, Bri?"

"Just for a sec. Before the game at his locker."

"So tell me, what's he like?" He could see her smiling as her face looked back at them from the rearview mirror. "Is he at least as cute in person?"

"*Mom.*"

"Oh," she said. "I've been hit. Somebody help me. I've been Mom-ed."

Brian said, "He doesn't say very much."

"Like my batboys tonight."

"I guess," Brian said.

Finn said, "Same."

She officially gave up then. When they got home after dropping off Finn, Brian said he wasn't ready to sleep yet. His mom told him she was cool with that and joked that both of them were moving up on having vampire hours. Before she headed upstairs, she said, "Hon, seriously? Did something happen at the game that you're not telling me about? With Hank or anybody else? Did you do something wrong?"

Yeah, he thought, I did. I tried to talk to my hero. But he wasn't going to tell his mom that. So he just said, "Guess I'm already taking these losses too hard."

Then he added, "But you know what they say, right?"

"What do they say?"

"Long season."

If it worked for the players and coaches and the manager, why not for him?

He poured himself a glass of milk and went into the den, where he used to watch games with his dad.

Now the den belonged to him when there was a ballgame on he wanted to watch. He turned on ESPN's *Baseball Tonight* and waited for them to get around to Hank Bishop's return to Comerica, something they teased through two sets of commercials.

Finally they got around to the Tigers highlights. There was Hank's second-inning single, several shots of the Comerica crowd on their feet cheering him, one guy holding up a huge sign that said, "The Bishop of Baseball Is Back!" Then came a brief shot, very brief, if-you-blinked-you-missed-it shot, of Hank acknowledging the crowd by tipping his cap.

He was interviewed on the field after the game by one of the ESPN reporters, saying to the woman, "Until we lost the game, I felt like I was walking on air."

You *were*? Brian thought.

His mother had come back downstairs without Brian hearing her, but he heard her now from the doorway, turned, and saw her holding her own glass of milk, staring at Hank Bishop's face on the screen.

"Like I said in the car," she said. "Cute."

This time Brian didn't say anything.

"Killer smile."

"Yeah," Brian said. "It's killer all right."

CHAPTER 8

Brian and Kenny were on the field at Way Elementary on Thursday morning with the place to themselves.

Kenny wasn't scheduled to pitch again until they played the back end of a two-game series against the South Oakland A's in Royal Oak on Sunday night. So he was treating today like his "throw" day, same as a big-league pitcher would, getting in some light throwing between starts. And when it was his throw day, he would bring a bag of old balls to one of the fields run by Bloomfield Little League and pitch batting practice to Brian.

When Kenny had first suggested a routine like this, Brian had told him it wasn't the job of the starting pitcher on the

Sting to help the part-time left fielder stay sharp at the plate.

But Kenny Griffin had his own ideas about being a bud.

"You're going to miss a ton of practice time," Kenny had said. "So you're going to need to get in your hitting against real pitching or you're going to have no swing at all. The real pitching would be me. End of conversation."

"Can I just say one thing?" Brian had said to the guy everybody knew was the best pitcher in the district.

"Go ahead."

"Please go easy on me."

They always watched how many pitches Kenny threw, and he got plenty of breaks, just like he was pitching real innings. Bag of balls after bag of balls. And they both figured out right away that it didn't feel like real practice at all.

Just pure fun.

Brian had caught a break with the Tigers' schedule that week. They were playing the Rangers in ESPN's *Sunday Night Baseball* game. So Brian could play the one o'clock game against South Oakland and still get to Comerica in plenty of time to get his work in before the eight-fifteen start.

At Way Elementary now Kenny said, "Three balls left."

They'd been going awhile and Brian was actually starting to get tired. Kenny never seemed to get tired. "I promise to groove all three," he said, "and give you a chance to hit one out."

"My arms are too tired, dude. I'll be lucky to get one through the infield."

"*You're* too tired?"

"I keep telling you," Brian said. "*You* have a rubber arm. *I* have a rubber bat."

"Shut up and hit."

"On it."

He came close to hitting one out with his last swing, groaning as the ball came up two bounces short of the wall. When they were through collecting all the balls, they stayed in the outfield, sitting in the grass in front of the narrow warning track.

"Things getting better with you and your he-ro?" Kenny said, swigging ice water from the jug he had brought with him.

"No," Brian said. "But they haven't gotten any worse."

"So he hasn't talked to you at all since the other night?"

"It's like I'm not even there."

Kenny said, "What's he like with the other players?"

Brian laughed. "Pretty much the same."

After just three days Brian had noticed that Hank did more talking to the media in front of his locker every afternoon than he did to his teammates. Brian would always make sure not to stop and stare when he was in the clubhouse. As he went about his normal work, he'd see Hank smiling his famous smile and answering the reporters' questions, and he began to think of it all as some part in a play Hank was playing.

Because as soon as the reporters were gone, Hank would lean his bat against the wall of his cubicle and disappear into the trainer's room to lie down on one of the tables, or go into the players' lounge and be by himself a little more.

It was pretty clear that Hank Bishop could be by himself almost anywhere.

"He seems like such a great guy when you see him get interviewed on TV," Kenny said.

"Maybe I should get a notebook or a microphone and act like I'm interviewing him," Brian said.

"My dad says that you're better off *not* knowing these guys," Kenny said. "He says that way you're not disappointed when you find out they're not who you think they are. Or who you want them to be."

Brian said, "I'll let you know who he is when I get to know him."

"*If* you get to know him."

"You make a solid point," Brian said.

All he knew so far, just watching Hank Bishop in action both on and off the field, watching pretty much every move he made as often as he could, was this:

More than anybody in that clubhouse, from the batboys

all the way up to the manager, Hank Bishop looked like this was a job to him, a job Brian wasn't even sure the guy liked anymore.

After everything that had happened to him, after all the time he'd been away from baseball, what must have seemed like a lifetime even though it was less than two years, Brian had just assumed—maybe like a dope—that Hank would be happier than anybody to be back inside this world.

Only he wasn't.

It never felt like a job to Brian, like real work.

The constant cleaning up after the players, the never-ending call for more Gatorade and coffee. Running new baseballs to the home-plate umpire at record speed during the game. Grabbing a new bat for one of the players who had broken one, getting *that* out there at record speed. It was all a game to Brian. Already he had learned the certain sound a bat made when a baseball broke it, and he'd be heading down the dugout steps for a new one before the player even completed the walk over. Then Brian would dash over to gather the broken pieces of bat. He'd learned early how sharp those pieces could be, cutting himself on one of the shards. Even that Brian didn't mind.

After the game there was the sweeping up. The dugout usually looked like it had been lived in by twenty-five of the biggest slobs in the world. And the bats needed to be organized. And everyone's shoes shined.

None of it felt like work to Brian. Not with this kind of backstage access.

Brian loved it when a foul ball ended up in his area. He'd pick it up and be the one who got to toss it to one of the kids, sometimes his age, sometimes younger, reaching over from the stands, having brought their gloves to the ballpark the way he used to. For that one moment, while he decided where to toss it, while the kids all yelled, "Over here, over here, *here here here*," he'd feel like one of the players. He had the ability to make somebody's night.

He'd make mistakes sometimes, usually when trying too hard to please. He made one with Hank Bishop one day, trying to do him a favor—do his job—and getting in trouble for it. It was after a game and he saw Hank's bat in front of his locker, just lying there on the rug. He went over and picked it up, intending to take it down to No. 3, when he heard Hank's voice behind him.

"Where are you going with that?"

Brian turned around.

He'd thought Hank was gone.

"I was just going to put it with your other ones in the equipment room."

"That's one of my gamers. It must have fallen out of my locker," Hank said. "My favorite bats always stay in here.

Always." He gave Brian a look that made him feel like the dirt around home plate. "Unless you were planning to sell one of them on eBay."

He must have seen Brian's face fall—crumple was probably more like it—when he said that, because he added, "Just let it sleep there from now on."

Brian stood there, silent, like a bat rack.

"You're excused, batboy."

"My bro," Willie Vazquez said when he spotted Brian one day. "Get your skinny butt over here."

Brian was almost relieved to see that Hank Bishop wasn't sitting next to Willie in front of his own locker. No. Not *almost* relieved.

Brian *was* relieved.

Willie handed Brian two twenty-dollar bills. Then in a low voice he said, "Bro, I *got* to have some real food. I can only take so much of Davey food. *Birds* eat better than ballplayers now, least in here."

Davey Schofield had gotten big on healthful eating after the team had faded down the stretch the season before. So before a game, the only thing laid out for the players on the buffet table in their lounge was fresh fruit and vegetables.

"Real food?" Brian said.

"Bro, lower your voice!" Willie said. "You're a guy. I got

to have some greasy guy food. I got to draw you one of those Happy Meal pictures?"

"Mickey D's," Brian said, almost in a whisper.

Willie slapped him five. "What I'm *talkin'* about!" he said. "There's one you must've seen, about two blocks up toward the Ren Center."

"What do you want?"

"Two quarters with cheese, one Big Mac, double fries, one of those little apple pie deals," Willie said, grinning. "You got yourself some leeway picking out the main course."

"The main course?" Brian said.

"I'm just playin'," Willie said. "Maybe throw in one of those chicken sandwiches. Just don't stop ordering till you use up the money."

Brian looked around. "You want me to bring it back here?"

Willie said, "*Hale* no, my brother. Where do you and the little freckled dude dress?"

"Equipment Room No. 3," Brian said.

"I know where that is," Willie said. "Meet you there in twenty."

Not only did they meet there in twenty, but that's how much Willie tipped Brian when they were alone in front of Brian and Finn's lockers.

Finn showed up just as Willie was finishing up. The skinniest player on the team had eaten everything except one bag of fries. And even though he was through eating, Willie seemed in no rush to leave.

"Ask you somethin'?" he said. "How you two getting along with the Bishop?"

Brian wasn't sure how to answer that, since Willie and Hank lockered right next to each other. He looked at Finn, who shrugged and said, "He's a little hard to get to know."

"I hear you on *that,*" Willie said. "It's like he's been mad at everybody so long, he doesn't know how to stop. He doesn't act like he's hatin' on the press, but even they know better. He just wants to be on their good side on account of so many of them jumped ugly on him when he took the fall on the steroids."

Brian said, "How do you get along with him?"

Willie smiled now. "I'll loosen him up 'fore the year's over. 'Cause if I can't? Nobody can."

He looked at the last bag of fries now, still sitting there, untouched, between Brian and Finn. "You gonna finish those?" he said.

Brian watched Willie inhale the last of the fries and thought of a quote he'd found on the Internet one time, when he was researching a paper on Jackie Robinson. Roy Campanella, who'd have a terrible car accident later and end up paralyzed, had been the catcher on the same Brooklyn Dodgers teams that Robinson had played on after breaking baseball's color barrier in 1947. And Campanella had been a great player, too, described as the fastest guy to ever play catcher in the big leagues. And one time Roy Campanella had said, "You have to have a lot of little boy in you to play this game."

Willie Vazquez had enough for the whole American League. He stayed with them a little longer, doing his impressions of some of the other players, Hank included, mocked their pitching styles and their batting styles and even the way some of them walked. He had them laughing so loud he kept telling them to hush or he was going to lose his secret eating place. Finally he said he had to go get ready for batting practice.

When he was gone, Brian found himself wondering if there was a way Willie could lend some of the little boy in him to Hank Bishop.

CHAPTER 9

The Tigers and the Angels, the first-place team from the AL West, were playing a crazy game tonight—one of those big, messy games where there was good hitting and bad pitching all night long and so many runs crossed the plate that Brian imagined the kind of sounds a pinball machine made every time he scored more points.

The Angels were ahead 8–4 in the sixth when Willie Vazquez hit the first grand slam of his career to tie it. The Angels scored three more in the seventh on a bases-loaded triple, Brian's favorite play in baseball, one where everybody on the field seemed to be running at full speed.

But the Tigers came right back with three of their own in

the bottom of the seventh to make it 11–11. Brian looked up at the scoreboard and nearly laughed: eleven runs and nineteen hits for the Angels, eleven runs and twenty hits for the Tigers. Three errors for each team.

A food-fight mess of a game.

There was even what felt like a record number of broken bats tonight. He kept hearing that broken-bat *sound* over and over, which meant he was running as much as the players. And the team had emptied the Gatorade cooler by the end of the seventh inning.

By the ninth inning, the score was 13–13. At that point Davey decided to bring in Brad Morley, his closer, even though it was a tie game. In a crazy game like this, Davey was banking on Morley getting him three outs without giving up a run, giving the Tigers a chance to score the winning run in their last ups.

But Morley was just one more pitcher who didn't have it tonight. He managed to get the first two outs on rockets hit to the outfield, both tracked down by Curtis near the wall in dead center. But then the Angels' catcher, Cal Stewart, timed a fastball perfectly and hit an absolute bomb over the left-field fence. Now it was 14–13. Morley got the next batter to fly out, but the damage had been done.

The Tigers were three outs away from an ugly loss. In came Todd Wirth, the Angels' closer.

Willie Vazquez, who had already scored two of the Tigers'

thirteen runs, led off with a walk, and advanced to third on the very next pitch when Curtis Keller singled to right field. The crowd was raucous now, practically shaking the stadium. But a three-pitch strikeout of Mike Parilli followed by a first-pitch pop-up off the bat of Marty McBain to the third baseman had let most of the air out of the balloon. Until everyone realized what they were about to see. It was something Brian had been waiting for all week. All his baseball life, really.

Two outs, bottom of the ninth. Hank Bishop at the plate with a chance to win the game.

Hank had scored a run earlier, but he had also struck out twice, including once when the bases had been loaded. Now, as Hank walked slowly toward the plate from the on-deck circle, Brian was afraid Davey might call him back and pinch-hit Bobby Holmes—go lefty hitter against right-handed pitcher.

Don't do it, Brian said to himself. Not against this guy.

Not against Todd Wirth of all people.

Davey must have been thinking the same thing because he never even looked in Bobby Holmes' direction. Just sat stoically, chewing on sunflower seeds as Hank stood in the batter's box.

And proceeded to whiff through two fastballs.

It was 0–2, just like that.

Brian, sitting at the edge of his chair, nearly fell right over on strike two. He had seen just this week that Hank had trouble catching up with real good fastballs now. But if he could just time one now . . .

He thought, You're still rooting for this guy as hard as you ever did, even knowing what he's like.

The ballpark grew louder again, encouraging Hank, wanting to be part of his comeback. Hank fouled off one 0–2 pitch. Then another.

"C'mon, Bishop!" Willie yelled down from third, clapping his hands. "Bring it home, baby."

Wirth delivered another fastball.

Brian knew not only the sound of a broken bat by now, but when a guy had connected. And Hank Bishop connected now—Brian knew it before he saw the high arc of the ball, knew from the sound the ball made on the fat part of Hank's maple bat.

The ball had been carrying in the hot air all night, even with no breeze blowing out to speak of, and now it carried Hank Bishop's moon shot to right.

Brian watched it the way everybody in the ballpark did, standing, including the rest of the Tigers, all of them at the top step of the dugout, with their heads back, eyes wide, watching the flight of the ball.

"Get *out!*" Davey Schofield yelled. *"Get out of here!"*

Jordy Hall, the Angels' right fielder, was running full speed, acting as if there were no wall in front of him. At the last second, in perfect stride, he timed his jump and climbed the wall, just inside the foul pole.

Then he came back to earth, ended up sitting in the dirt in front of the wall, and in that silent moment nobody at Comerica, including Jordy Hall, knew whether this was one of those "Web Gem" plays everybody would watch on the late *Baseball Tonight*.

Or if the Tigers had just won the game.

Jordy looked into his glove.

Nothing there.

It had taken a few extra seconds, but Hank Bishop had just hit a two-out, three-run, walk-off homer—his first home run since coming back to baseball—to win the game.

Brian raced for home plate like the rest of the Tigers, hanging in the back of the crowd waiting for Hank to finally reach home plate. After Willie touched the plate, he ran back up the third baseline to act as cheerleader, running along with Hank, then jumping on his back as Hank got ready to touch the plate himself.

Hank had enough memory and enough experience to toss away his batting helmet before crossing home, knowing he was about to get pounded on. It was the only show of emotion Brian had seen from him all the way around the bases.

Brian ran for the helmet. He had already had Hank's bat in his hand. Wasn't about to let go of either one.

And when the celebration around the plate was over and Hank had finished with his postgame interviews, first for the Tigers' television network, then for Tigers' radio, finally for ESPN and the MLB Network, Brian Dudley could no longer contain himself.

Not on a night like this.

He was waiting near the top step of the dugout, knowing that Hank liked to take his favorite bat, his gamer, to his locker with him, sure that this night wasn't going to be any different.

As Hank approached him, Brian said, "Your first homer in the majors, your very first one, was against Todd Wirth! How great is that, you did it again!"

Then he handed Hank the bat.

Hank nodded and took it. Behind Brian were all these people still in the stands near the Tigers' dugout, still cheering the home run, still cheering for Hank Bishop. Brian could hear the kids calling Hank's name, just wanting him to look in their direction. There was one kid, wearing a Tigers cap and a Tigers T-shirt, glove on his left hand, screaming, "Hank, this is the greatest night of my whole *life!*"

Hank didn't even look at the kid, any of the kids. But he did look at Brian with this look on his face that was almost curious, as if he didn't understand what Brian had just said to him.

"Fascinating," he said.

Then he took the bat from Brian and disappeared down the dugout steps.

Brian stood there for what felt like a long time. Even the kids who had been yelling Hank Bishop's name started to leave. Finally he took one last look into the stands. The kid in the Tigers cap was still there, watching Brian.

Almost like he knew.

Brian walked down the dugout steps, got one of the baseballs the home-plate umpire had thrown out of play in the ninth inning. Without a word, he came out and stuck it into the kid's glove.

Sometimes you wanted to go home with something more than a memory.

It was a lot more than Brian was going to get from Hank on this night.

CHAPTER 10

Mr. Schenkel called Brian and Finn into his office after Saturday's game, saying he had something he wanted them to tell their parents.

It was always "parents," Brian noticed. Plural. It was something you noticed when you had only one parent.

Singular.

"Okay, here's the deal," Mr. Schenkel said to them in his office. "There are going to be times this season when there's a real late game one night and a real early game the next day and the most sensible thing is going to be to just sleep here. So with ESPN making us their *Sunday Night Baseball* game and us having to play a twelve thirty on Monday because the Rangers are flying to the West Coast right after the game, well, long story short, we're gonna just stay over tomorrow night."

Brian wasn't sure he'd heard him correctly.

"Stay . . . *over*?"

Finn said, "No *way*."

"It's a fact," Mr. Schenkel said. "Now you can both close your mouths. I didn't tell you before because I didn't want the two of you to start pecking at me the first time a Friday night game ran late and we had to turn the whole thing around for Saturday afternoon."

"We get to have a sleepover . . . *here*?" Brian said.

"*If*," Mr. Schenkel said, "it's okay with your parents."

"Oh, trust us," Finn said. "It will be."

And it was.

Brian explained to his mom what Mr. Schenkel had explained to them: that Mr. S. would take the couch in Davey Schofield's office and Brian and Finn would sleep on the two couches in the main clubhouse, the ones set up in front of the two flat-screen television sets.

Liz Dudley shook her head. "By the end of the season *I'm* going to end up feeling like your home away from home."

"Do you not want me to do this?" Brian said, scared as soon as he said it that she might say that she didn't.

"No, no, no," she said. "You go and have a good time. I know it's where you want to be."

"It's only going to be this one night and maybe a few others during the season," Brian said.

She closed her eyes, slowly shook her head. "Look at me," she said, "getting to live the baseball dream all over again."

As she walked out of the room, she said, "It's like they say about the mob. Just when you think you're out, they pull you back in."

The last thing he heard was her shutting the door to her bedroom. He'd always known that baseball was never going to be anything he could share with her, not the way he had with his dad when he was still around. And he'd tried to tell her every way he knew how that baseball wasn't ever going to come between them the way it had with her and his dad.

But now he wasn't so sure.

First he got two hits against Royal Oak, even plated the go-ahead run in the seventh when he doubled home Will Coben, before the Sting scored six in the eighth to turn the game into a total beatdown.

When the game was over, he changed in the car, his mom

getting him down to Comerica at four o'clock on the nose, yelling at him as he sprinted for the entrance that he'd forgotten his gym bag, the one with his toothbrush and a change of clothes in it.

"Thanks," he said, out of breath.

"I have never seen anybody this excited to get hardly any sleep," she said.

He went straight for Willie Vazquez's locker, the way he did every day now, starting to feel a little bit like he should be wearing one of those little red McDonald's outfits as he took Willie's order. By now, word of the burger runs had spread, and Willie gave him orders from Curtis and Mike Parilli, too.

"Mike, too?" Brian said.

"He says he'd rather eat paper than those little cut-up veggie deals," Willie said. "Just think of it as givin' us all fuel, just with pickles and fries and whatnot."

And tonight it worked like rocket fuel for Willie. He went 4-for-4, scored three runs, knocked in three, stole two bases, and even ended the game with an acrobatic play behind second base—laying out to his left, somehow gloving the ball, then flipping it out of the glove in one motion to the second baseman, who made the turn like a pro and finished off the double play that gave the Tigers a 7–5 win over Texas.

Then the night became different from all the others before it. Usually Brian was in no hurry to finish his chores, even when he knew his mom or Finn's mom would be waiting outside. Sometimes even Finn would tell him to pick up the pace, asking Brian if he was shining the shoes or putting new soles on them. Mr. Schenkel liked to tell Brian they didn't have all night.

Tonight they did.

The game had taken three hours and thirty minutes, which meant that the game-ending double play didn't come until a few minutes before midnight. Brian saw the players showering and dressing in a hurry, dumping out of the clubhouse as quickly as they could, knowing they had to be back by ten in the morning, even though Davey had given them all a shout-out that there wouldn't be any batting practice.

Hank Bishop, who'd hit another home run tonight, was usually one of the first to leave, which made it easier for Brian and Finn to stay out of his way once they started doing their work—staying out of what Finn called the line of fire. But for some reason he took his time tonight, ended up being one of the last to head for the players' parking lot, actually pausing to say "'Night" to Mr. Schenkel as he passed by his office. As usual he ignored Brian and Finn, who were tossing towels and uniforms into a bin near the clubhouse doors.

It wasn't until Hank had disappeared through the doors that Finn sarcastically said, "Good game, Hank."

Brian joined in. "We'll have your coffee ready when you get back, just the way you like it."

Finn, laughing now, said, "Hope I don't spit in it."

"Heard that!" Mr. Schenkel called out from his office.

Then they all laughed, Brian and Finn the loudest, mostly because it was still totally ridiculous to them that they got to do this tonight.

When all the work was done, Mr. Schenkel brought out a couple of dark-blue Tigers blankets and a couple of pillows, then began shutting off the lights in the players' lounge and in the trainer's room.

"Ask you something, Mr. S.?" Finn said.

"Where are your cookies and milk?" he said.

"No," Finn said. "I wanted to ask if we can watch TV for a little while."

Mr. Schenkel handed them the remote. "Knock yourselves out," he said. "Just keep the volume down, because I'm going to be asleep in about ten minutes."

Brian and Finn had each brought T-shirts and the Tigers sweatpants Mr. S. had given all the batboys. They changed into them now. "It's like we're getting into our jammies," Finn said, before Brian told him to shut it.

Now the only lights in the clubhouse came from the flat-screen in front of them, showing all of the highlights from Sunday's games.

When the show went to a commercial, Brian got off the couch and walked over to Hank Bishop's locker.

"Be careful," Finn said. "There might be some sort of invisible fence around it, like people use for dogs."

"Just want to check it out," Brian said.

Hank had a couple of bats in there, a few extra pairs of spikes, a pair of sneakers. A pair of jeans hung on a hook. There was a bunch of toiletry stuff on the upper shelf.

And taped to the inside of one of his locker walls was a picture of a girl.

A teenaged girl, Brian was guessing, tall and pretty, smiling, standing on a beach somewhere.

The picture was big enough that she had written "Love you, Daddy" in Magic Marker against the blue water behind her and the blue sky.

Brian had almost forgotten that Hank Bishop had a daughter. He'd gotten divorced during his steroids suspension. Brian suddenly remembered her name, Katie. Katie Bishop. Living near an ocean somewhere without a parent, singular, the way Brian was.

He stood there and stared at the picture and wondered if there was one like it in the clubhouse of his father's team in Japan, because Brian had sent him one earlier this year without telling his mom he was doing it, a picture of him and Kenny in their Schwartz Investments Pirates uniforms. He'd included a letter along with the photo, telling his dad about his season, about his batting average and RBI.

Told him at the end how much he loved him and missed him.

And never heard back.

Brian had no way of knowing how old the picture of Katie Bishop was, how long ago it had been taken. He stared at it now, and for some reason, it made him like Hank Bishop more.

CHAPTER 11

It was past midnight now, way past, on the night of the great Comerica sleepover.

"C'mon," Finn said, "they're about to show the plays of the week on the Tigers' channel."

"Plays that occurred," Brian said, turning, "in a ballpark we are still inside of."

"Good night, children!" Mr. Schenkel yelled from behind the closed door to Davey Schofield's office.

"Good night, Mr. Schenkel," they sang out in classroom voices.

They watched the highlights from the week. Watched Willie's four hits, his headfirst slides on his steals, watched him glove that ball behind second again. Watched the replay of Hank's walk-off against the Angels again, saw the other players jumping him at home plate. It wasn't like the rockets he used to hit, Brian knew. It looked more like a ball just falling out of the sky, landing just beyond the right-field wall.

Who cares, Brian thought. The swing still looks the same, just not the results. There had been a fly ball early in tonight's game, one that the crowd thought was a home run when it came off Hank's bat. But when it ended up an easy out on the warning track, Brian had heard the Rangers' pitching coach yell out, "Not anymore, big boy." Trash talk about the steroids.

Brian didn't know whether Hank had heard, but Brian had.

They watched the rest of the highlights until Brian looked over and saw that Finn had fallen asleep, as if the air had come out of his balloon all at once.

Brian gently took the remote out of his hand and used it to shut off the television. He left Finn where he was and took the other couch, the one in front of the other television set. The only light in the Tigers' clubhouse now was from the supermarket-style refrigerators, the ones with the glass doors and bottles of water and Gatorade and fruit juice and Vitaminwater inside, the ones he and Finn were constantly restocking.

He was almost ready for sleep, too. Almost. But first there was something he wanted to do. He walked across the room, through the double doors, down the stairs, and up the runway to the dugout.

Then up the stairs to the field.

He took it all in. The quiet expanse of the outfield. The blue tarp on the mound at home plate. He noticed that the lights at the top of Comerica were dimmed slightly, and would stay that way through the night.

Then he walked over to home plate in his bare feet, feeling the cool, wet grass underneath him, and got into the batter's box side. He took a huge swing with an imaginary bat, hit himself a great big imaginary home run, and started to run around the bases, taking his time.

As he came around third, he tossed away an imaginary batting helmet before jumping hard on the blue tarp covering home plate.

He took one last look around, taking in the sights of the empty place and the night sounds, even though there were hardly any sounds at all at this time of night. Comerica was so quiet he could actually hear the hum of the stadium lights.

He started back toward the dugout, again feeling the soft ballpark grass underneath his feet.

When he got to the top of the dugout steps, he used his

own chair as a ladder and hopped into the stands and walked up through the empty rows and then over a couple of sections to the two seats on the aisle where he and his dad used to sit, in the last row of Section 135.

And in that moment, Brian didn't feel alone at all.

CHAPTER 12

Hank Bishop was the first player there the next morning, arriving in the clubhouse a few minutes after Davey Schofield.

And for the first time, Hank spoke to Brian without Brian saying something to him first.

"Hey," he called out when he saw Brian across the room.

Brian couldn't help looking over his shoulder to make sure he was the one Hank was talking to, even though it was just the two of them in the clubhouse. Brian was there to make sure the coffee had finished brewing and was ready for the early arrivals.

There were two forty-two-cup Hamilton Beach coffee urns set up on a long table in the clubhouse for regular coffee and a smaller pot for decaf, because only Davey Schofield and Rube Morgan, the old pitching coach, drank decaf. One of the urns had an *R* on it, meaning "regular." The other had an *H*. For "high test."

The high test was like the coffee version of Red Bull, which meant a caffeine bomb. Brian and Finn had been instructed to put twice as much ground coffee into its oversized filter—going by Mr. Schenkel's instructions—as they did the other.

And to make sure it was always filled, even after the game had started.

"Sometimes our kids need a little jolt to get their hearts started," is the way Mr. S. put it.

But Brian knew enough about major-league baseball to know the deal, had read up on how players dealt with the long season. Many of them used to use amphetamines before amphetamines became a banned substance in baseball, something you got tested for along with other illegal drugs like the ones Hank Bishop had used.

The players weren't kidding anybody. Brian knew high-test coffee was a kind of substitute now, even if nobody talked about it that way.

"Hey," Hank said now. "Hey, you."

You, Brian thought.

"How about a cup of your breakfast special?"

High test.

"Yes, sir," Brian said.

He filled up a tall cup, not having to be told what kind of coffee he drank because he still watched every move the guy made without letting on that he was watching.

Brian walked the coffee across to him, eyes on the cup the whole way, desperate not to spill any.

"Here you go, Mr. Bishop," he said, handing it to him.

Hank Bishop tasted it, winced a little. Brian stood there as if waiting to be dismissed. "Yep," Hank said now. "My favorite. Kind that tastes like you ought to be pumping it for three dollars a gallon at the gas station."

"Is it *too* strong today?" Brian said.

Thinking he'd already said more than he should have, even about a stupid cup of coffee.

Hank Bishop said, "Let me explain something to you: It could *never* be too strong to suit me."

He placed the cup on the carpet next to him, Brian noticing even more bats than usual inside his locker today. Then he picked up the sports section of the *Free Press* he wanted waiting for him at his locker before day games. Brian could see his eyes scanning the front page. Then Hank looked up, as if surprised to see him still standing there.

"What's your name again?" he said.

Brian told him.

"Brian," Hank said. "Why can't I ever remember that?" Then he stood up with his coffee and his newspaper and headed for the players' lounge.

"Brian," he said again, without looking back.

And as much as Brian felt like a complete idiot, he turned and felt himself smiling as Hank disappeared through the door to the lounge. As he did, he saw Mr. Schenkel watching him from outside his office, shaking his head, almost like Brian had done something wrong.

"What did I do?" Brian said.

"*You* didn't do anything," Mr. S. said. "I just wish guys like *him* were nicer."

"Most are."

"Just not him."

"Not yet," Brian said.

"You ever hear the one about the guy who finally stops beating his head against the wall?" Mr. Schenkel said.

"No."

"When he finally does, somebody asks him how he feels and he says, *Great!*"

"That's me?"

"Little bit," he said. He shook his head. "I can't figure that guy anymore. He used to love every part of this game when he was a rookie. Almost like *he* was a batboy."

"Maybe he just forgot how," Brian said.

Mr. S. said, "I keep thinking the kid I used to know must still be inside him somewhere, but I'll be doggoned if I've been able to find him."

Then he held up the pair of shoes Brian hadn't noticed him holding in his hands, shoes looking scuffed and dirty, and said, "Somebody forgot to make Willie's kicks look pretty," and handed them to Brian. "Maybe a task like that will wipe that goofy grin off your face."

"Nah," Brian said.

It was as if both teams had forgotten to set their alarms for baseball today, and everybody was sleepwalking through the early innings of the game.

The Tigers scored three unearned runs in the second thanks to a booted ground ball and a throw practically into the stands, it was so far over the first baseman's head. The Rangers came back with four of their own, all of *those* unearned, in the top of the fourth when Marty McBain, with two outs, just flat missed a routine fly ball. No sun to speak of, no wind. He just lost concentration and closed his glove too early and the ball popped out. It was the kind of mistake even Brian didn't make when he was playing left field for the Sting at Kenning Park. The Rangers followed with five straight base hits and it was 4–3.

The Tigers got the lead back an inning later when the Rangers' pitcher walked four straight guys with nobody out and then allowed a sacrifice fly to bring in another run before Hank helped him out by grounding into a double play.

But then the Rangers' cleanup man hit a two-run homer to put them back on top, and that's when the game—and the players—finally settled down. Bottom of the eighth inning, Rangers 7, Tigers 6. One out, runners on second and third.

Hank Bishop up to bat.

A base hit would put the Tigers back ahead, a fly ball would tie the game. There wasn't much of a crowd for the afternoon game, but the people who were in attendance pumped up the volume now for Hank, who used to make his living in late-inning situations like this.

On the first pitch to him Joe Apuzzo, the Rangers' All-Star setup man, busted a cut fastball in on Hank's hands and broke his bat. Brian watched it happen, half the bat flying toward third base, and couldn't believe what he was seeing. Not because he hadn't seen anybody break a bat before, but because it was the fourth bat Hank had broken today, which in Brian's time as Tigers' batboy was more than any player had broken in a single game.

Hank usually had two of his bats in the dugout and three more in the rolling bat rack in the hallway. Then he had his complete stash, a dozen more, boxed in Equipment Room

No. 3, where all the Tigers had their extra bats, ones he hadn't tried out in batting practice or a game yet.

So Brian knew something Hank probably didn't, that he was down to his last good *game* bat.

He wanted to watch this at-bat, especially if Hank did something great here. But he couldn't take the chance, not with Joe Apuzzo being famous for breaking bats on right-handed hitters with that cutter of his knifing in on them when he had it working.

As if on cue, before Brian was down the dugout steps, Joe Apuzzo put another cutter on the inside corner and Hank made a defensive swing, fouling it off.

Brian heard the sound and winced. Hank's *fifth* broken bat of the game.

Now Brian was on the dead run, knowing he was already in trouble. Hank was going to be expecting him to be walking toward him with a new bat.

Brian could have stopped at No. 3, but he decided to run back to the clubhouse instead, taking the steps three at a time, having remembered the extra bats he'd seen in Hank's locker before the game. They were still there, underneath the picture of Hank's daughter. He grabbed one now, feeling like this was another kind of game and the clock was about to run out on him, feeling his heart pounding in his chest. He ran back to the dugout, up the dugout steps, nearly colliding with Davey Schofield as he did.

Feeling like Willie Vazquez flying around third base on a single and trying to score.

He was out of breath but grinning.

"You broke too many today," he said, handing the bat to Hank.

Hank grabbed the bat by the handle, both hands on it, whipped it back and forth in front of him. Over his shoulder Brian could see the home-plate umpire watching both of them, arms crossed.

The first rule of being a batboy, he knew, was to not delay the game. But he wasn't as worried about the ump as he was about Hank Bishop, because something was clearly wrong.

"What's this?" he said.

"Your bat. From your locker. One of your gamers. I noticed you had extra today."

"Who told you . . . This is the bat I was trying out in BP. It's way lighter than the one I usually use."

"But I thought . . ."

"You *thought*?" Hank said. "Thought about what? This is the wrong bat, you idiot."

Now Brian saw the home-plate umpire walking toward them, looking the same way he did when he was about to break up a conference at the pitcher's mound.

Brian didn't know how much time had elapsed, how much real time, since Hank had broken his last bat. It just seemed like forever.

"Problem, Hank?" the ump said, mask in hand.

"No," Hank said, glaring at Brian, walking toward home plate, taking some vicious practice swings as he did.

Brian went back to his chair, thinking that of all the times in his life when he'd rooted for Hank Bishop to get a knock when the game was on the line this way, he'd never rooted harder than right now.

Hank swung at the next pitch, as hard as he could at a cut fastball that didn't cut and seemed to hang right over the middle of the plate.

Popped the ball up, right to the shortstop.

He ran a few feet down the line, stopped when the guy caught the ball, walked calmly back to home plate, picked up the wrong bat with two hands, and broke it over his knee as if he were snapping a No. 2 pencil.

Then walked toward Brian, each hand holding half the bat, the last broken bat of the day.

Brian stood up and just waited for whatever was going to happen next.

When Hank got close enough, he spoke in a voice that only Brian could hear.

"If a batboy can't even handle bats," Hank Bishop said, "then what's he doing here?"

CHAPTER 13

Hank never got up again that game. The Tigers went down 1—2—3 in the ninth and lost.

Only Brian had heard what Hank said to him after he'd ended the last chance the Tigers had to come back. Maybe the bat had nothing to do with his missing a fat pitch. Or maybe just worrying about the bat had made all the difference.

Brian didn't know and didn't care.

This was on him.

It was like a bat *store* in that equipment room. And the room was closer than the clubhouse. Why hadn't he gone there instead? And why hadn't he thought of doing that sooner, the batboy who took such pride in being one step ahead of the game and always prepared?

He knew the answer. He *knew*. It was because he was trying too hard to make Hank Bishop like him, to wear him down and win him over.

Maybe even remember his name.

He'd thought there was something special about those bats in Hank's locker, even though Hank hadn't gone back during the game to get one for himself.

So Brian had done that for him.

He felt like the jerk now, felt like he'd cost the Tigers this game even if only he and Hank Bishop knew why. Unless Hank went to Mr. Schenkel and Davey Schofield or even the reporters and told them about the batboy who couldn't manage to put the right bat in players' hands.

Maybe, Brian thought, maybe Hank had been right from the start. Maybe everybody would be better off if Brian *didn't* talk to him or have anything to do with him.

Finn kept asking what was wrong after the game. Brian rolled with a version of things he'd used with his mom that time, the first day he'd met Hank, telling Finn that maybe he just took these losses too personally and too hard. They were in the dugout, sweeping up the trash and then putting it into Hefty bags, the real grunt part of the job, like being forced to clean your room at home.

"I don't believe you," Finn said.

"Believe me."

Finn said, "Dude? Don't take this the wrong way, but you lie about as well as my mom does when she tells me I'm not getting something for Christmas I know I am."

Brian laid his broom against the bench and sat down where Davey did during games when he got tired of standing on the top step. "I messed up today," he said. "Big time."

Then he told him.

When he finished, Finn said, "He blamed *you* because *he* didn't get a hit? That's worse than weak. That's like practically *dead*."

"He didn't come right out and blame me."

"Yeah," Finn Simpkins said. "He did."

"It doesn't matter," Brian said. "I can't do anything right with him, no matter how hard I try."

"You mean you're not like all the other close friends he's been making since he showed up here?"

"Bottom line? It was the wrong bat."

"They used to say he could go up there with a hockey stick and hit line drives," Finn said. "Remember?"

Brian did.

Then he took the broom, handed Brian the Hefty bag, and said, "Blame the batboy. Wow. What a guy."

They finished up in the dugout, went back to the clubhouse, collected the last of the dirty clothes, and put them in the laundry bin for Mr. Schenkel. Shined all the shoes, Hank's included. Then went back to No. 3 and changed into their regular clothes.

Brian wouldn't even look at the storage area where the players' extra bats were stored and stacked and organized by numbers, lowest to highest—rows and rows of them in shelves built into the wall.

He and Finn were being picked up separately today, Finn going out to dinner with his parents in the city. Brian's mom had the night off and they were going out to dinner, just the two of them, at the Townsend Hotel in Troy.

Before he left, Brian went back to the clubhouse for one last look. He wanted to make sure he hadn't missed anything, wanted to make sure he at least got things right *after* the game. The room was quiet, empty. Brian knew Mr. S. had to be around somewhere. Nobody with the Tigers worked harder than he did or put in more hours at the ballpark.

Yet Mr. S. was nowhere to be found. Even Davey and the coaches had beat it out of there by now, all of them getting the chance to have a night to themselves before the Tigers went back out on the road tomorrow.

Time to go.

Brian went back through the double doors, down the quiet hallway, pushed the button for the elevator, and heard it groan and start down from the lobby level. The doors opened. He got in. Then just as the doors started to close, he heard, "Hold the elevator!"

And in that moment he knew a bad day was about to get worse.

Because the voice belonged to Hank Bishop.

CHAPTER 14

"Thanks," Hank said before he saw who'd held the doors for him. Then he saw that it was Brian.

"Great," he added.

Brian thought, Took the words right out of my mouth.

"Do me a favor?" Hank said. "Don't apologize."

In a small voice Brian said, "Okay."

"Tell me you weren't waiting for me out here so you could apologize."

Brian, looking down at the floor, wanting to disappear through it, said, "I thought all the players were gone." Then added, "Mr. Bishop."

The ride to the lobby level took only a few seconds, but it felt longer today, one more part of Brian's long day, the one that had begun with a sleepover at the ballpark and was ending with a nightmare.

When the doors opened back up, Brian just waited for Hank Bishop to get out first. Which he did. Brian kept his mouth shut for once and put his head down and followed him, just wanting to get outside, get to the street, get to his mom.

But when he did get outside, Hank was waiting for him.

"Hold it," he said.

Brian stopped.

"I don't want to wear you out with this, kid," he said. "But you gotta leave me alone now."

"I didn't think I wasn't," Brian said. "Leaving you alone, I mean."

"I see you following me around," he said. "I see you watching me. But you gotta get it through your head, I'm not that guy. You think you know me. All you fans think you know me. But you don't."

His voice was rising, like he was getting mad all over again, like they were still standing there between the dugout and home plate, but this time Brian hadn't done anything.

"That guy?" Brian said.

"You know what I mean, don't act like you don't," Hank

Bishop said. "I'm not the guy you still want to be your hero. I was *never* that guy, even when I was going good. And you want to know something else? I never *wanted* to be that guy."

"I'm not asking you to be anything," Brian said.

Thinking, Except nice to me.

"Yeah, you are. You've got all this storybook . . . *stuff* going on. Like the writers do. Only this isn't a storybook. You gotta get that through your head. It's more than that with me. A *lot* more. You know why I came back *here*? You want to know the truth? There's only one reason I'm here. . . ."

He stopped himself then, as if he'd said way more than he'd intended to.

Or couldn't believe he'd said it to the batboy.

"I've got my reasons, is all," he said.

Brian looked up at him now, a voice inside his head telling him he was too big and too old to cry, as much as he wanted to. That if he started crying in front of Hank Bishop . . . well, that was something you *never* came back from.

"Why are you telling me this?" he said.

All the days when he couldn't wait to get to the ballpark, and now he didn't just want to leave, he wanted to *run*.

"Because I look at you and see what everybody wants out of me and I'm sick of it!" Hank Bishop said.

Brian didn't know what to say to that, now or ever. But he didn't have to worry.

"Well, well, well," he heard his mom saying. "If it isn't my favorite guy and his all-time favorite player."

He turned and saw his mom walking toward them, smiling her very best smile at both of them.

That wasn't the most amazing part.

The most amazing part?

That Hank Bishop, whose head had seemed ready to explode about thirty seconds before, was smiling back.

Brian said, "Mr. Bishop, this is my mom. Liz Dudley."

His mom, still smiling, said, "Heard a lot about you, Mr. Bishop."

"Call me Hank."

"I've heard a lot about you, *Hank*."

"Only the bad parts are true."

"Well, I find *that* hard to believe."

"Not if you heard the conversation I was just having with your boy."

"Did I miss something good?"

"Don't know if I'd call it good, exactly."

"Do tell."

She was still smiling, like it was some kind of show now near the employee entrance to Comerica Park.

"I was actually about to apologize to your boy before you came walking up."

"Apologize for what?"

"For jumping up his . . . For jumping *down* his throat for a mistake he made today."

Yeah, that was about to happen, Brian thought, him apologizing to me.

"I don't know as much about baseball as I should," his mom said then, "even having been married to a major-league pitcher. But isn't that the way you learn, from your mistakes?"

"You were . . . ?" Hank said to Liz Dudley. Then he looked over at Brian, like seeing him for the first time. "You never told me your dad pitched in the big leagues. What was his name?"

"Cole Dudley."

"You're Cole Dudley's kid? How come I didn't know that?"

Because you never even asked what my last name was, Brian thought, *that's* why. But he said, "I don't make a big deal out of it."

"I faced him when he was at the end of his career. Guy still had nasty stuff, even when he could barely break 80 on the gun. What's he doing now?"

"Pitching coach. Japan."

Hank looked back at Liz Dudley. "You and Cole Dudley . . . ?"

"Divorced," she said, and then as if Brian wasn't there, she said, "I was released with a full pardon."

"Wish I could have gotten one of those when I got divorced," Hank said. Now he was smiling again. "The same way I wish I could have learned from *my* mistakes.

"Anyway," he continued, "I'm glad you're around to hear me tell Brian I'm sorry I lost my cool before. You've got a great kid, Mrs. Dudley. . . ."

"Liz."

"You've got a great kid, *Liz*. Even though I haven't told him that yet to his face."

Brian actually thought he might choke on that one. This was the kind of performance Hank gave every day in front of his locker for the writers, the guys he said bought into the same stupid storybook stuff that Brian did.

They chatted a few minutes more, almost as if Brian wasn't even there. Hank said how nice it was to meet her. His mother said, "Nice to finally meet *you*."

Hank turned to Brian. "See you tomorrow?"

Brian just nodded.

Then, most amazingly of all, Hank put up his hand so that Brian could give him a high five.

"No hard feelings?" Hank said.

"No sir," Brian said.

No feelings at all.

Later, lying on his bed, staring at the ceiling in the dark, hands behind his head, unable to sleep, he couldn't believe what had happened.

He'd thought about telling his mom the truth at dinner, but stopped himself. What was the point? Maybe if she thought Hank Bishop was a good guy, she'd like baseball a little more. Or at least hate it a little less.

He just couldn't believe what he'd witnessed outside Comerica. When Hank Bishop finally tried to act like a human being, it was toward Brian's mom. The mom who suddenly decided it was a fun fact that she had been married to Brian's dad, someone she could usually go months without mentioning.

I've heard a lot about you, Hank.

You've got a great kid, Liz.

Gag me, Brian thought.

CHAPTER 15

The Tigers were scheduled to play two games in Minneapolis against the Twins. Then they were going from there to Chicago for three against the White Sox. After that they returned to Comerica for a ten-game home stand against the best of the American League East: Rays, Red Sox, and Yankees.

What that meant to Brian was that he got a full weekend of baseball with the Sting, Friday and Saturday games against the Lake Orion Dragons, then a doubleheader against Motor City on Sunday at Lahser High School.

He still missed the team when it went on the road, missed the routines he'd already fallen into in a pretty short time, for both day games and night games. He even missed hanging around with Finn every day.

But the idea of taking a little break from Hank Bishop didn't kill him.

He knew this wasn't just his summer with Hank Bishop, it was his summer with the *Tigers*. That meant the other twenty-four players, the manager, the coaches, Mr. Schenkel, even the broadcasters he saw at the ballpark every single day. He'd been given a kind of backstage pass to big-league baseball.

Not to just one guy.

Even if that one guy had been his favorite player his whole life. And even if that one guy seemed to be taking over his life. Now even his mom seemed interested in baseball.

On Thursday night she came into the den and announced she was going to watch the Twins game with him, at least until *Grey's Anatomy* came on.

"I'm sorry," Brian had said when she'd sat down in the big leather chair in the den that used to be his dad's favorite seat for watching baseball. "Are you *lost*?"

"*Lost* is Wednesday night," she said.

"Good one, Mom."

"What," she said, "I'm not allowed to watch a little baseball with my boy?"

"You mean watch something you *never* watch?" Brian

said. "Or maybe it was one of my other moms who told me once she'd rather have food poisoning than watch a whole baseball game? The mom who just the other day was comparing baseball to the *Mafia*."

"Those were figures of speech," she said. "In writing, we call it dramatic license. Even newswriting. And, by the way, I didn't say I wanted to watch the whole game."

"You just want to watch Hank," he said.

"Maybe I do, maybe I don't."

Like they were still just kidding around. Only now Brian wasn't. He didn't know why the air in the room had changed, why he felt hot all of a sudden. But he did.

"You meet the guy one time and suddenly you're interested in the Tigers?"

"And there's something wrong with that?" she said. "I thought you wanted me to like baseball."

"Mom," he said, "when I first got this job, you sounded like you'd rather have me be a bag boy in a supermarket than a batboy for the Tigers. Or mow lawns to make extra money. Or just hang around the house doing nothing."

"I come in and want to watch a few innings of a game with you and now you're getting *mad* at me?"

"I'm not mad."

"Well, you sound mad to me."

"Well, I'm not."

She turned the chair a little, angling it so she was facing him now.

"Then I guess I'm not getting this," she said. "Because you're the one who told me one time that I shouldn't hold baseball against you because of the problems it caused for me and your dad. And for you."

"I know I did. But, well, you shouldn't like baseball again just because of this one guy, is all."

"But I thought he was your guy," she said. "Are you telling me now that he's *not*?"

"No," he said, "I'm not telling you that."

"Then what are you telling me? I feel like we're having a fight about something here and I don't even know what it's about," she said. "Which *is* something I mastered when your dad was still around."

"I guess I'm just saying that I don't get you sometimes."

"Makes two of us," she said, getting up out of the chair now. "If you don't want me to watch with you, just tell me and I won't."

"I'm not saying that, either."

"Okay, then."

"Okay." Brian sighed, trying to squeeze a smile out of himself. Trying to change the air. "Hank just struck out to end the top of the second. I'll call you when he's up again."

"Okay," she said, and walked out of the room.

Brian sat there thinking. It was as if Hank Bishop was in the room even when he wasn't, when he was playing on the road, because he was up on his mom's radar now. And that *was* making him mad, even if he wasn't going to admit it.

Liz Dudley had an expression she used on Brian all the time: Be careful what you wish for. Now he knew exactly what she meant. Ever since his dad had left, there'd been so many nights when he sat in this room and wished he had somebody he could share the games with. Now he wasn't so sure. By the time Hank Bishop did come up the next time, he was up in his room, listening to the game on the radio. Alone. And liking it.

Alone and wondering how baseball ever got this complicated.

Brian sat there thinking. It was as if Hank Bishop was in

The Sting won both games at Lake Orion's home field, Brian's only hit of the series driving in a run. It was Will Coben's ninth-inning home run that won Saturday's game.

They ended up losing the first game of Sunday's double-header against Motor City, but that wouldn't be the game everybody would remember. The second game, with Kenny Griffin pitching, was the one they'd remember at Lahser High.

It wasn't going to decide anything in their league, so there was no reason for the game to have any kind of playoff juice or edge to it. But the longer it went on and the longer it stayed scoreless, the more it felt *exactly* like the playoffs.

Brian felt the way he did watching Tigers games from his seat next to Davey Schofield, only this was better. This was what Kenny called "the goods." This was a great game that Brian was *in*.

He had worried that because he had the batboy job, playing for the Sting might not make him feel the same way he used to about playing ball. But he was finding out today on the field at Lahser High that there was nothing to worry about. He was actually glad the Tigers were in Chicago today because if they hadn't been, he would have missed out on Bloomfield–Motor City, Game Two.

From the top of the first, Kenny had pitched like the total star he was. His pitch count was low today, as low as Brian could remember it. He had been around the plate all day and the Motor City hitters weren't taking many pitches, almost like they wanted to keep Kenny out there as long as possible, even as Brian could hear their coach practically begging them to be patient.

Kenny usually had to be pulled from the game once the seventh inning ended because the maximum number of pitches he could throw—the number agreed upon by his dad and Coach Johnson—was ninety. And he'd be right around ninety by the sixth or seventh. But today the innings kept going by fast and Kenny kept getting stronger, striking out the side on eleven pitches to end the Hit Dogs' seventh.

"You good?" Coach Johnson said to him when he got back to the bench. "Because you're only at sixty-eight pitches."

"Sixty-six," Kenny said, toweling off.

"Well, I got you with two more."

Kenny grinned at him. "All due respect, Coach? I got *you* two off."

"I take it that you'd like to continue then?"

"Try getting the ball away from me."

"What we need to get is a run."

It came in the bottom of the inning, Kenny doing the job himself, singling home Will from second with one out and then advancing to second base on the throw home. Brian had a chance to make it 2–0 when he ripped the first pitch he saw from the Hit Dogs' starter, a beast of a lefty with a vicious rising fastball. But the ball hung up just enough in right-center for their center fielder to run it down.

So the game stayed 1–0 headed into the eighth. Kenny got two quick ground balls and a strikeout to close out the top of the inning. He was still way under his limit, but Coach Johnson came over and sat next to him with the Sting up to bat in the bottom of the eighth. Before their coach even asked the question, Kenny grinned at him and said, "Coach? Don't even think about it."

It actually made Coach Johnson laugh. "Coaching this

team is such an easy job sometimes," he said, and got up and walked away.

When he was out of earshot, Brian said, "You sure you're good?"

Kenny turned to him and in a whisper said, "I'm gassed. Totally. *Mad* gassed. But you know the deal. This is my chance to go the distance. Never did it in Little League, never did it in school ball." He kept his voice low and said to Brian, "You know that home run you want to hit someday? Going nine is that home run for me. A tape-measure shot."

Brian knew exactly what his bud was talking about. The Sting went down in order, so Kenny didn't get much rest before taking the mound for the top of the ninth. He walked the first batter he faced on four pitches, took a deep breath, then got the second batter to line out to Will at first.

The ball was hit hard, though. The next kid singled on the first pitch.

First and third, one out. And Brian could see that Kenny was laboring out there.

"C'mon, finish these guys," Brian said to himself, willing the words to reach Kenny all the way from left field.

The next batter worked the count full and should have taken ball four to load the bases, but he wound up doing Kenny a favor by swinging right under the high pitch.

The runner on first had been running with the pitch and ended up stealing second easily.

One more out to go.

Brian hadn't been doing the math, but if Kenny wasn't at ninety pitches by now, he was close enough as the Motor City cleanup hitter stepped into the box. He was the biggest kid in the game, and strong. Brian had heard the other kids calling him "Buddha," not sure whether the nickname was meant to be a compliment or not.

Thinking, It sure does fit, though.

Buddha had hit the ball hard every time he'd been up, even if he still didn't have a hit to show for his efforts.

Inside, Brian said to himself. Do *not* let him extend those massive arms.

Inside, Kenny G.

The first pitch wasn't close to being inside. Not only did Buddha extend his arms, but he got all of the pitch, hitting a hooking line drive toward the left-field line.

Hard to Brian's right.

And this ball wasn't going to hang up like the one Brian had hit earlier. Buddha had gotten on top of Kenny's fastball, putting all this topspin on it, like the killer forehand in tennis.

Getting a good jump on the ball wasn't Brian's strong suit as an outfielder. He had a strong arm, and if he could get his glove on the ball, he could catch it. But he wasn't fast and he knew it.

He'd been ready for this one, though, and got a good jump

on it. Still, he felt his heart sinking the way the ball was, the ball tailing away from him too hard and too fast, Brian just knowing it was going to land fair. And if it landed fair, both runners would score and the Sting would lose. And Kenny would have finally gone nine, only to lose the game.

Brian waited until he couldn't wait anymore and went into his dive, extending his left arm across his body, lying out with his glove hand as much as he possibly could.

He felt two things then, one right after another.

He felt the ball in the webbing of his—what else?—Hank Bishop glove.

Then he felt his right shoulder hit the outfield grass at Kenning Park as hard as if he'd used that shoulder to try to break down a door. But Brian wasn't worrying about that, he was just worrying about keeping his glove as high above the grass as he could, even if that meant his shoulder had to take all the impact when he hit.

So he didn't roll. It was basically as if he'd just belly-flopped out there, about a foot from the chalk of the left-field line.

But with his Hank Bishop glove high enough for the in-field umpire to see.

The glove that held Kenny's first complete game ever in its webbing.

Brian sat up, holding the glove above his head now, like

some kind of trophy. The ump signaled out. Brian sat right where he was and saw Kenny, still standing on the mound, throw his own glove up in the air.

Then he watched as his bud ran toward the Sting's bench, where Kenny's father was pumping his arms in celebration. They hugged, hard.

Brian stood and began slowly walking off the field, his shoulder suddenly hurting a lot more than it had a moment ago.

CHAPTER 16

There were so many questions he wanted to ask Hank Bishop, so many questions he realized he would probably never get answers to.

It was pretty clear by now that Hank wasn't just rusty at the plate. Even Brian could see that he didn't have the same bat speed he used to have.

There was something else, too. Brian couldn't pinpoint what it was, exactly, but something about Hank's swing itself looked different. Brian told himself it was just the angle he had, now that he was watching on the field. But even watching from home when the Tigers were on the road, there was no denying it. Hank Bishop was no longer the hitter he once was.

Brian remembered Tim McCarver one time on the *Game of the Week* saying that getting a fastball past Hank Bishop was like getting table scraps past a hungry dog.

Now Brian wished there was some way to ask him what that was like. What it felt like to swing and know instantly that the ball was headed out of the park for a home run. What adjustments he had to make at the plate now that his hands wouldn't do what he wanted them to do, what his brain was probably still *telling* them to do.

And did it make Hank mad?

Or maybe just sad.

Hank Bishop wasn't a bad hitter now. He just wasn't great anymore. His average was at .280 since he'd come back to the Tigers, with three homers and ten RBI. But whether Brian was watching him from next to the dugout at Comerica or watching him on television, he'd always see a few pitches per game that were practically begging to be crushed by Hank's bat but would end up being routine fly balls.

More than anything, though, the question he knew he would never have the courage to ask was this:

How much Hank Bishop thought steroids had to do with the success he used to have.

Brian loved baseball enough to know that it was the re- cord books, the *stats,* that connected one era to another, that connected somebody like Ty Cobb, the greatest Tiger of them all—and, from everything he'd read, a hundred times the jerk that Hank could be—to the players of today. And Brian knew that what was now called the "steroid era," the era that pretty much took up his whole life, had made a fine mess of the record books and of history, especially when it came to home runs, because nobody could sort out how much the modern stats were real and how much they had to do with drugs. Who was clean and who wasn't.

Every time one of Hank's balls ended up on the warning track, he wondered if it would have been a home run five years ago.

He knew Hank had to wonder the exact same thing, whether he'd ever admit that or not.

Brian had experienced a lot of feelings since Hank Bishop became a Tiger again, more bad than good. A *lot* more bad than good, actually.

He'd never expected to feel sorry for him. Yet he did.

Even stranger, in a way that Brian couldn't understand properly, it made him feel sorry for himself.

It was three thirty in the afternoon, middle game of the Red Sox series, halfway through the home stand, the Tigers riding a four-game winning streak, and Brian and Finn were in Equipment Room No. 3, the real start of their day.

"Here's what you need to do, if you want my opinion," Finn was saying.

"Wait a second," Brian said. "This opinion, the one you're about to give me, is this one I have a choice about?"

"Yes," Finn said. "But I'm telling you in advance, it's not one you'd want to miss out on."

They were changing out of their own clothes and into their Tigers golf shirts.

"I'm going to risk it," Brian said.

"I know you well enough already to know you don't mean that," Finn said.

He turned now, having pulled his shirt over his head.

"You gotta stop thinking you're going to get to know Hank the Crank," Finn said. "Get to know what he's *really* like."

He put air quotes around *really*.

"Why's that?"

"Because *this* is what he's really like!" Finn said.

"I still don't believe that," Brian said.

Finn acted as if he hadn't even heard him. "And I've got another bombshell for you."

"Wow," Brian said. "Who's luckier than me today?"

"All those questions you tell me you want to ask him about being a former juicer? Say you did ask him one day in a moment of complete wigged-out insanity. You think he'd give you an honest answer? He still won't admit he even *took* the drugs, remember? Says he didn't know what his trainer was giving him."

"I still want to know."

"Dude," Finn said. "You're the big history guy, remember? You're the one who told *me* that guys wouldn't tell the truth about drugs even when they went in front of *Congress*."

"Yeah. Mark McGwire said he didn't want to talk about the past on a day all they *wanted* from him was to talk about the past."

"You need to start focusing on the guys who actually like having us around," Finn said. "Not Hank the Crank, who acts like *we* were the ones who suspended him from baseball."

Brian thinking: The guy acts like he's *still* suspended.

Hank was playing in the field tonight for the first time since coming back, playing third base. Brian knew he was ready for it even though all he'd done was DH so far, having watched Hank take ground balls at third every single day during batting practice. He had even seen him take grounders at first, breaking in a brand-new first baseman's mitt, a surprise just because Brian knew without looking it up that Hank had never played a game at first base in his entire professional career.

The bigger surprise? Being in the field was something that seemed to make Hank happy. Brian would stop and watch him during practice making one clean, smooth pickup after another, making one sure throw after another across the diamond. And those simple actions would actually make him smile sometimes, even get him to engage in a little light trash talk, nothing heavy, with Willie Vazquez, the king of trash talk with the Tigers.

"Ooooh, Mr. Hank Bishop," Brian had heard Willie say today after Hank had backhanded a ball behind third and fired a strike across to Bobby Moore at first. "I didn't know your arm was still *so* strong and powerful."

And Hank had said, "Compared with your rag arm? Yeah, I guess mine would look powerful."

Willie had laughed like that was the funniest thing he'd ever heard, then laughed again a few minutes later when Hank ranged way to his left and cut in front of Willie to pick up a grounder that was practically in Willie's glove. But instead of throwing to Bobby Moore, Hank just took the ball out of his glove and, in what seemed to be one slick motion, went behind his back with it to Willie, who had the presence to barehand the ball and gun it to Bobby himself.

The two of them high-fived each other and, watching from the dugout, Brian thought that maybe these few minutes were the start of something. That maybe going back in the field tonight might make Hank feel more like the player he used to be.

It was almost a rough beginning, though. He nearly booted a ball in the top of the first when the ball caught the edge of the grass before the infield turned to dirt. The ball jumped on Hank, came up and caught the heel of his glove, falling in front of him. But he was able to grab it with his bare hand and make what Brian thought was a pretty amazing throw and to get the runner by a step.

When the Tigers came off the field, Davey Schofield put out his hand and said, "Nice recovery."

Hank said, "I used to be able to field balls like that with my *teeth* and not drop them."

In the top of the fourth, two out and two runners on, full count on the Red Sox cleanup hitter, Hank made the defensive play of the game. The runners were going with the pitch and the batter hit a screamer that bounced over the bag, but somehow Hank was there. He timed his dive perfectly, came up out of the dirt with the ball, and threw what looked like a 95 mph fastball to get the out.

As Hank came off the field to a standing ovation, he did something Brian couldn't remember his having done since his first night back at Comerica:

He tipped his cap.

Another good sign.

Maybe.

Tom MacKenzie, the Tigers' starter, had been the biggest fastball phenom in baseball before three shoulder surgeries robbed him of his heat. He was a ground-ball pitcher now, getting by on a lot of sneaky off-speed junk. But tonight, throwing his sinkers and changeups, he induced batter after batter to beat the ball into the ground for easy outs. Through seven brilliant innings, he had given up just one run to the high-powered Red Sox offense.

The problem was, despite runners on base in just about every inning, the Tigers couldn't score at all. So the game stayed 1–0, Boston. You didn't see many of those pitching battles in the American League, the league with the designated hitter.

Between the top of the seventh and the bottom, Finn came running down to the dugout to get a quick drink and said to Brian, "You know when you told me that a 1–0 game could be, like, the best?"

"You mean the time I told you and you answered that I was an idiot?"

Finn said, "I take it all back. Because this is . . ."

"Baseball," Brian said, just because sometimes that explained everything.

The game was still 1–0 Boston in the bottom of the ninth when Willie laid down a perfect bunt single against the Red Sox closer, Rex Green, known through baseball as T-Rex because he was 6 foot 6 and weighed 266 pounds. On a thin day.

T-Rex was known for ignoring base runners, so Willie proceeded to steal second on him. T-Rex came back by striking out Curtis and then Marty McBain. But Bobby Moore walked. So did Mike Parilli.

Bases loaded, two out. Hank Bishop walking to the plate. Brian heard Davey Schofield behind him, saying, "Well, here's your Hollywood ending."

Tom MacKenzie might have been pulled from the game an inning ago, but he hadn't left the dugout, not even to ice his shoulder. Now he was standing next to Davey.

Brian moved his chair a little closer to them and heard Tom say, "He has trouble now catching up to this kind of cheese."

"I just got a feeling," Davey said. "Had it all night."

Tom said, "Davey, if one of us is gonna be right, let's have it be you."

The count went to 2–2. T-Rex had a splitter, but he was strictly going with what Tom called his cheese now—his fastball. High cheese. Hank had swung through the first two fastballs but laid off the next two, both of which were high and outside the strike zone. Brian was expecting another fastball, thinking T-Rex wasn't going to take a chance getting beat on his second-best pitch.

But that's exactly what happened. He must have thought he could cross Hank up, get him off balance, maybe even sneak that splitter across the inside corner for a called strike three.

Hank wasn't crossed up at all. He was sitting on the pitch

as if he knew it was coming, and just the sound of the ball on the fat part of that maple bat told Brian he had gotten all of it. That he still knew what to do with a mistake pitch like that.

That was the only sound Brian needed to know the ball was gone. Not only would this be a walk-off home run, but it would be a *grand-slam* walk-off. Number 499 for Hank's career—just one away from the magical 500.

He jumped to his feet like the rest of Comerica and watched Hank Bishop instead. Hank knew it, too. He took two steps out of the batter's box and stopped, posed really, flipped the bat away, watching the flight of the ball.

He had gone to right-center with this one, gone the other way, the way he used to when he used the whole park, when he had power to all fields. His swing still didn't look the same to Brian. But he had sure put an old-time, Hank Bishop crush on the ball.

And everyone in the stadium was standing as one, waiting for the ball to clear the wall.

Everyone except Tony Gilroy, that is, the Red Sox center fielder, who was running toward the wall in right-center. He slowed at the warning track, reached up casually without having to jump, and gloved the ball about two feet shy of the wall.

Game over.

Red Sox 1, Tigers 0.

Hank Bishop was still standing between home and first when Gilroy came sprinting toward the infield with his glove held high in celebration.

Brian couldn't see Hank's face, but he saw the way his whole body seemed to sag. He wondered which was greater: the shock that the ball hadn't been a home run. Or the humiliation that he'd been so sure that it was.

He didn't walk toward the Tigers' dugout right away, just turned around and walked slowly toward the place in the grass where his bat had landed.

Just as Brian got there to pick it up.

"Don't touch it," Hank Bishop said in a quiet voice.

Brian looked up at him.

"I got it," Hank said, then reached down and picked up the bat as if that took all the strength he had.

Brian didn't know what to do next, so he just followed Hank Bishop across the field. When Hank got to the dugout, he walked down the steps but didn't head for the clubhouse, just took a right turn and went to the far end and sat down, placing the bat next to him.

Finn's voice was a whisper. "What do we do now?"

Brian whispered back. "Work around him."

So they did, staying away from Hank, cleaning up as best they could. They removed the coolers, came back and collected the towels, took the other bats out of the rack and stored them in Equipment Room No. 3.

They got back to the dugout and saw that Hank Bishop was still there, still staring toward the outfield.

Brian and Finn were in the runway, trying to decide what to do about sweeping up with Hank Bishop still there, when Mr. Schenkel walked past them and saw Hank for himself.

"Leave the rest of it," he said. "I'll take care of it later."

They did. Left Hank where he was.

On the night when Brian was sure he had turned himself back into the old Hank Bishop, Hank just looked old.

CHAPTER 17

It wasn't just Hank who wasn't the hitter he used to be.

Brian had completely lost his stroke for the Bloomfield Sting. Forget warning track power—he had *no* power now, and he couldn't buy himself a base hit. The harder he tried, the more clueless he felt.

Kenny had a theory about it. But then Kenny Griffin had theories about everything from whether or not space aliens actually existed to palate expanders and how they had just been invented by kid-hating orthodontists for their own sick, twisted amusement.

"You know whose fault your slump is?" he said. "The Tigers'."

"The *Tigers'*?"

Kenny nodded, the way teachers did when they led you to the right answer.

"Yup. You spend so much time with them and so little time with us, you're picking up bad habits. Despite the fact that you spend most of your days and nights watching guys with *excellent* habits."

"You know what my bad habit is?" Brian said. "Striking out."

"It's just a slump."

"More like an incurable disease. Terminal scrub-ness."

They were back at West Hills, getting ready to play the third game of three against the other team from Rochester, the Bulldogs. The two teams had split the first two. Brian had struck out three times in Friday night's loss and three more times yesterday, a game Kenny had saved with a two-out, two-run single in the bottom of the ninth.

"I've got one more theory," Kenny said.

"You always do."

"I think maybe you're a little burned out."

"Burned out," Brian said, nodding like he was agreeing. "At fourteen. Good call. Burned out. Why didn't I think of that?"

"Go ahead and go full snark on me," Kenny said. "But check it out: Maybe even *you* can't eat, sleep, and drink baseball every single hour of every single day of your whole life."

"So this *isn't* the Tigers' fault," Brian said. "It's *baseball's* fault?"

"Now you're talking."

"And you're a freak," Brian said. "This isn't baseball's fault, it's my fault. I couldn't hit a meatball right now with a fork."

"Meatball with a fork? Dude, I gotta admit, that's the first time I ever heard that one."

"It's one of Davey Schofield's. He's got a lot of them. One time he referred to a play as being the straw that broke the coffin's back."

Kenny laughed, which didn't take much. Sometimes Brian wondered if he was ever sad about anything besides giving up a run.

"You know when you're snapping out of the junk?" Kenny said. "Today."

But Kenny was wrong. The Sting might have won the game, but Brian went hitless, striking out three times in four at-bats.

The more he pressed, the worse it got. The more he guessed on what pitch was coming, the dumber he looked. He was either off stride or late getting his hands through or pulling his head off the ball on every pitch.

The only thing he was consistently hitting right now was *air*.

When it was over, even though the Sting had won in a beatdown, his mom consoled him, or at least tried to, as if they'd lost the game.

"Tough day, pal."

"You *think*?"

"You'll get 'em next time," she said.

They were walking toward the parking lot. Brian knew she was just trying to be a mom, even if she didn't know the right thing to say.

Brian stopped.

"Please don't," he said.

"Don't what?"

"Don't act like you know that things will get better," he said. "Kenny tried that earlier. Because you *don't* know. I'm lucky to even be *on* this team, and now I'm the one doing the most to let it down."

"Sorry for trying," she said. "But then, I was never much good at pep talks even if I do know a thing or two about persistence."

"Mom," he said, "let's not do this today."

"I wasn't aware we were doing anything."

It didn't matter what the subject was these days, Hank Bishop or anything else, all these conversations were starting to feel the same. Sound the same. He stood there between the field and the parking lot trying to remember the last time talking to his mom felt easy.

It was as hard as trying to remember the last time hitting a baseball felt easy.

"The sorry one is *me*," he said, and started walking again

toward their car. "Maybe if I can't be a real member of the team, then I shouldn't be on it anymore."

"I don't know what to tell you, kiddo," his mom said.

Finally she was right about something.

"But I have one more thing to say, and I think you'll want to hear it."

Brian steeled himself and faced her.

"Your father is coming to town."

CHAPTER 18

Dad?" Brian said. "Coming *here*?"

"He arrives on Thursday. He's apparently in the States to do some scouting for a week or so. He said that originally he was supposed to stay on the West Coast, but now—isn't this a happy coincidence?—they want him to take a look at Hank Bishop with an eye toward maybe bringing him to Japan next season."

"Hank . . . Japan? No way. Even I know he's way too proud."

"Your father says that he's still a huge star over there and that they've signed guys like him at the end of their careers, for a lot of money."

"So, am I . . . are we going to see him?"

"He wants to come here the day he arrives, says he's going to the Tigers game that night, leaving the next morning."

"He's coming to a game?" Brian said. "Does he know . . . ?"

"About your job?" she said. "He does, as it turns out. Because when I gave him the news, he informed me that you'd informed *him* in a letter."

"I tried shooting him an e-mail," he said, "but it bounced back. I figured Dad's still as computer savvy as ever."

His mom said, "It's not the contact info I'm interested in. I wasn't aware that there was any contact at all."

Brian wasn't going to take any heat—have his brand attacked, as Kenny would say—for telling his dad he'd gotten a batboy job. So he just tried to make a joke out of the whole thing. "Technically," he said, "if somebody doesn't respond, then how much contact did you really have?"

Now she smiled for real.

"You got me there," she said. "I'll give you more details on this breaking story as it comes in."

He wasn't going to tell her this, but the only detail that mattered was that his dad was coming to town. Brian knew he'd take any kind of contact he could get with him.

Even if it was for only a day.

Cole Dudley hadn't changed all that much. Starting with the fact that he still seemed to think that a high five was the same as a hug, no matter how long it had been since you'd seen your son.

Brian and his mom and dad were in the living room and Brian was still trying to process the fact that the three of them were in any kind of room together. But they were until his mom—who acted as if she'd rather be anywhere else in the house except here—finally said, "Well, you two have some catching up to do and I have to get ready for work."

Before she left, Brian's father asked, "How's that going for you, at the station, I mean?"

"It's going," she said, and walked out.

His dad's hair might have a little more gray in it. He might have put on some weight, Brian wasn't sure. But he didn't really look any older than he had when he'd left. He had worn a blue blazer to the house, and when he took it off now and draped it over the back of the couch, Brian saw that his golf shirt had "Chiba Lotte" stitched on it.

"It's great to see you, pal," he said.

"You too."

His dad was on the couch now, Brian in the chair facing him, on the other side of the coffee table. He hadn't known where to sit and had just grabbed the chair.

"Listen," his dad said, "before we talk about anything else, I'm sorry . . ."

And that was as far as he got. What hadn't changed about his dad? It still looked to Brian as if he had the biggest hands in the world, hands that could make a baseball disappear as if he were doing some kind of magic trick with it. His dad stared down at those hands now, as if he'd rather have a ball in them, as if then he'd know what to do . . .

"Dad, you don't have to."

"No, I do. I'm sorry about the way I left, sorry that I haven't called or written back or anything." Now he looked up. "But getting out of here," he said, "it was like when it was time to get out of baseball. Pitching-wise, I mean. It was just time, is all. I didn't want to stay around and try to find the right words, or answer the questions I knew you'd want to ask. If it had been a game, I'd have just handed you the ball like I was taking myself out and kept walking."

He smiled at Brian, and then shrugged. "Anyway, I'm real glad to see you, as hard as that might be for you to believe."

"Dad," Brian said, "you don't have to explain now. Really, you don't."

He worried in that moment that if he said the wrong thing, his dad might get up and leave again, before his one day with him had even started.

His dad, still smiling, said, "Gee, but I'm so good at it." He nodded at the doorway. "Practiced my talking skills with your mom's back."

There was a quiet between them now, neither one of them

sure where to take this next. Brian thought, All the times when I wanted to be with him watching a game on TV, or sitting next to him in Section 135, and now here he is and I don't know what to say to him.

And he knew why. Knew how little they'd *ever* had to say to each other when they weren't talking baseball.

"So the batboy deal," he said. "They being nice to you?"

"Yeah."

"You like it then, being around the game every day?"

"A lot."

"They know you're my son?" he asked. "Even if you probably don't feel like that lately."

"Some of the guys do," Brian said. He grinned and said, "You know, the older ones."

"Ouch."

Then it was quiet again. Brian could hear his mom moving around upstairs, the floorboards squeaking the way they had since they'd moved into this house, when they were still a family.

"What about you?" Brian said. "How's the Japan deal working out?"

"Well, they sure do love their baseball," he said, "so I'm good with that. Not so good on the food, of course, the raw fish and whatnot. So I feel like I spend a lot of my free time looking for a good burger."

"You like coaching?"

"Oh, I still have a lot to say on the subject, but now I've got to say it through a translator. Though some of my own old coaches would say I always needed one of those."

"You were always good at talking baseball to me, Dad," Brian said.

First time he'd called him that today.

Dad.

"Well, I can tell you it's a little different over there," his dad said. "'Cause once I get past *konnichiwa* for hello and *sayonara* for goodbye, I pretty much got to use these old hands of mine."

Brian could see him loosening up now, relaxing, settling into this, always more comfortable talking about himself, about baseball. "It's good honest work and better than anybody was offering me in the big leagues. And it helps that I'm working for an American."

Bud Valley had managed the Twins and the Orioles in America, but had taken the job with Chiba Lotte after the Orioles had fired him two years ago.

"Bud must trust you if he's got you scouting now," Brian said. "Mom said you want to take a look at Hank Bishop."

"Your man," his dad said. "Oh, I don't think I've got a snowball's chance in Miami of even getting him to talk to us when the season's over. But they surely would pay him, because he's the kind of big American name they love over there." He grinned again and said, "Heck, you don't even have to be a big name. Some of them even remember your old man."

He sighed. "But enough about me," he said. "You really doing okay, pal?"

I'm still his pal, Brian thought. Talking to me like I'm still five, when he'd come home for a visit during the season, about this time of year, or come home for good after the season, before he'd find some excuse to get to Florida or Arizona early for spring training. . . .

"Good," Brian said. "Really good. I really do love my job, and I was even having a pretty good season for my team, the Sting, before I went into this horrendo slump."

"Man," his dad said, "aren't those the pits?"

"My swing feels all discombobulated, like I'm off balance all the time."

His dad nodded and Brian knew what he wanted to happen now, wanted his dad to tell him they should go find the nearest field and he'd take a look at it.

His dad's cell phone went off. Still playing "Take Me Out to the Ballgame." He pulled it out of his pocket, looked at the number, said, "Gotta take this, pal," and walked through the terrace doors to the small outside patio. "Yeah, I'm in Detroit, on my way to the ballpark in a little while, then out of here on the first flight tomorrow."

The conversation didn't last long; they never did with his

dad. When he came back inside, he said, "Hey, I was think-ing, we got some time here before I drive you to Comerica."

"*You're* taking me?" Brian said.

"I cleared it with the boss," he said, pointing upstairs.

"*Cool,*" Brian said.

"Like the old days," his dad said. "Just the two of us."

Maybe it was going to be a great day after all. "Yeah," Brian said. "Like that."

"Anyway," his dad said, checking his watch, "we still got a little time and I'm starving. How about we get some lunch?"

"Sushi?" Brian said.

"Funny," Cole Dudley said. "I want to find a thick burger dripping so much blood it's like I just shot it myself. Is Hunter House still in business over there on Woodward?"

"Sure is," Brian said.

"Let's get out of here," he said. "Go get ourselves a couple of big, fat sliders."

One thing really hadn't changed with his dad, then.

He still couldn't wait to get out of this house.

CHAPTER **19**

His dad had called ahead to the Tigers and they had given him a seat in the stands where some of the other scouts sat. Tonight, for the Tigers–Blue Jays game, the seats were on the home team side of the park, but closer to home plate than the Tigers' dugout, in Section 130.

Not exactly the old seats, but close enough.

Cole Dudley had told the Tigers' PR people that he was coming with Brian, so they left his ticket at the Montcalm entrance, along with a one-day media credential that would get him into the Tigers' clubhouse and onto the field.

His dad had said on his way to the ballpark that he wanted to say hello to Marty McBain, his old teammate, and Rube

Morgan, the ancient—or so Brian thought—Tigers pitching coach. Brian had never really talked with Mr. Morgan, but it turned out that he had been Cole Dudley's first pitching coach in the majors, when he'd come up with the Dodgers.

And his dad had mentioned that he'd pitched with Tom MacKenzie when MacKenzie was a phenom in Boston, and with Mike Parilli for two months in Arizona once.

He had never played with Hank Bishop, but Brian knew that Hank's lifetime stats were great against Cole Dudley: twenty career at-bats, ten hits, three home runs, eight RBI.

"I told them in Japan that if they were looking for references on Hank, they didn't have to go any further than me," his dad said.

Everybody made a big fuss when his dad walked into the clubhouse. Bobby Moore, who'd played a year in Japan once, even bowed and said, *"Konnichiwa,"* and Brian's dad laughed and said, "I got your *konnichiwa* right here, dude."

And just like that—that fast—Brian's dad was one of the boys again.

Or maybe once you were one of the boys, once you were in the club, they always treated you that way. Maybe it was like the Robert Frost poem they were studying in English, the one about home being the place where when you went, they had to take you in.

Davey Schofield came out of his office to say hello, and Marty McBain lifted up Cole Dudley in a bear hug, saying that his old buddy sure hadn't missed many meals over there. Mike Parilli told him to save a job for him. Tom MacKenize joked that after all his arm surgeries, now *he* knew what it was like to get by with total junk, the way Brian's dad had his whole career.

"Junk and brains," his dad said.

Tom said, "If it was brains, you wouldn't have lasted long enough to earn your pension."

They all laughed again.

The only one not making a fuss, not included in the reunion, was Hank Bishop, who was just sitting in front of his locker signing the balls in a box that would be passed around the room eventually so everybody on the team could sign them. Brian knew that this box was on its way to the Children's Hospital of Michigan.

Hank would look up occasionally and take the scene in, the way Brian was. Like he wasn't a part of it.

The way Brian wasn't.

When they'd first entered the clubhouse, Brian was at his dad's side, standing there, grinning as people came up to him. At one point his dad had even said to Marty McBain, "You better be watching out for my kid."

Something his dad hadn't done himself in a long time.

"He's a great kid," Marty had said. "Best batboy we've ever had. Knows the game, too. Must get that from his mother's side of the family."

Then he and Marty began reminiscing about the time when their plane had been grounded by fog in San Francisco and they'd had to hop a bus back to Los Angeles, and how one of the rookie infielders was in the bathroom at some diner and got left behind.

Almost without realizing he was doing it, Brian had moved away from the scene in the middle of the clubhouse, was standing near the door to Mr. S.'s office. He knew he had work to do, he couldn't just hang around all day.

But even though it was as if he'd moved out of the picture, been cropped out of it, he couldn't make himself leave.

At one point he saw his dad go over, say something to Hank, shake his hand. Hank nodded, no expression on his face, looking at Cole Dudley the way he would at Brian or Finn. His dad reached into the side pocket of his jacket, pulled out what had to be a business card, and handed it to Hank. Looking more like a salesman in that moment than an ex-player.

Rube Morgan finally came through the door in his uniform, gave his dad a hug, and said, "I don't know what's in the water over there or them Californy rolls, but you look older'n *me* now."

"Rube," his dad said, "only the earth is older than you."

"But you *do* look as if you could still give me a third of an inning."

"Oh man," Cole said, "don't I wish."

"Listen," Rube said, "I wish I could catch up with you, but we just called up some twenty-year-old kid from Triple A and I've got to go see what kind of stuff he's got. You want to come?"

Cole said, "You don't have to ask twice."

Then Rube Morgan was telling him about the kid's minor-league statistics and the two of them walked right past Brian, his dad not even seeing him, and out the clubhouse door.

Brian watched them go. Watched the door close behind them. *Sayonara,* Brian thought. He leaned against the wall outside Mr. Schenkel's office, feeling tired all of a sudden, even though he hadn't done a stitch of work yet, hadn't even changed out of his regular clothes.

There was a lot less noise, a lot less action, in the clubhouse now that his dad was gone. Somebody turned up some music.

Still Brian didn't move. When he finally pushed off the wall, he felt himself sag a little, felt that catch in his throat you felt when you started to cry. He closed his eyes, swallowed hard, stopped what was trying to come out of him right there. He hadn't cried when Hank Bishop had started yelling at him on the street that day, and he wasn't going to cry now because his dad had made him feel as if he were invisible.

But he did need to get out of here.

Now.

Brian took one last look across the room, to the spot in the middle near the couches where his dad had been meeting and greeting before he'd left for the bullpen with Rube Morgan.

And noticed Hank Bishop staring at him.

Brian looked up into the stands in the top of the fifth inning and saw his dad sitting with the other scouts at the game, pointing at something in the outfield, smiling and saying something to the guy sitting to his left, both of them throwing back their heads and laughing.

There was a pitching change going on and Brian didn't have anything to do, so he looked over at Section 130 for a long time, waiting for just one look back from his dad.

Look at *me*, Brian thought, down here on a big-league field, in a big-leaguer's uniform.

But it was as if he wasn't here, the way he hadn't been in the clubhouse. It was as if he didn't matter to his dad, whether he was at Comerica or on the other side of the world.

He finally snapped out of it when he heard the home-plate umpire yelling over to him, saying, "Batboy!"

Brian's head whipped around, but he saw the guy was grinning at him, hands on hips, mask tipped back, saying, "Earth to . . . ?"

"Brian."

"Sorry, Brian, I got no head for names. Could you go grab me my bottle of water?"

He went and got the bottle of water where he kept it for home-plate umpires on a shelf in the dugout, and then went back to work, knowing exactly what he had to do.

They said their goodbyes outside the clubhouse about fifteen minutes after the Blue Jays had beaten the Tigers and the media was already inside talking to the players.

"You're sure you don't want me to wait and take you back?" his dad said.

"No, I'm good," Brian said. "I never know how long it will take to finish my work, and Finn's mom is coming anyway."

"I thought maybe we could go out and grab a bite before I dropped you home."

"Dad," Brian said, "ballplayers go out to eat after games, not batboys."

"Well, I'm glad we got to go to another ballgame together," Cole Dudley said, "even though it was a little different than it used to be."

"It was great to see you, Dad."

"Yeah. You too."

"I'll check in once in a while, let you know how I'm doing," Brian said.

"I promise to do better with letters," his dad said. "Even thinking about buying myself a laptop finally. Then we could e-mail each other."

"Right."

"Well, you take care of yourself," he said, then added, "and your mom."

"She's pretty good at taking care of herself."

"Always was," Cole Dudley said. "Always was."

A couple of writers, late coming down from the press box, went past them. Brian and his dad stood there, out of words before they were out of time.

"Next time I'll try to stay longer."

"That would be *great*," Brian said.

They looked at each other.

Then his dad put up his hand for a high five and Brian gave him one and walked quickly back toward the dugout, leaving his dad there, not looking back.

Finn was collecting towels.

"Hey," Finn said.

"Hey."

"Where you been?"

"Just getting things straight with my dad," Brian said.

"Everything cool?"

"Totally."

Then he got busy pulling bats out of their slots, not wanting to talk about a day with his dad that had ended up crushing him, even though he was sure his dad thought everything was fine. Brian realized now that it was too late for his dad to be somebody else, to be the dad Brian had been holding out hope he could be.

He turned around and saw Finn looking at him and thought of something his mom liked to say, that sometimes guys had to talk about stuff whether they wanted to or not.

As usual, he ignored that voice.

He and Finn split up their chores the way they always did, Brian taking on most of the shoe-shining work tonight, Finn helping Mr. Schenkel get the laundry started since there was an afternoon game tomorrow. When they were finished, Brian took one last walk-through in the dugout to make sure they hadn't missed anything.

When he got back to the clubhouse, Mr. Schenkel was turning out the lights in his office. "Trying to make this an early one, because tomorrow's an early day," he said. "Lucky we got a fast game in tonight."

"I was thinking the same thing," Brian said.

"You and Finn good to go?"

Brian nodded.

Mr. S. said, "You guys want to walk out with me?"

"I left a couple of things in No. 3," Brian said.

"It was nice seeing your dad," Mr. S. said. "He seemed pretty happy to be with the guys."

"Yeah," Brian said, "he loved seeing the guys."

"Well, tell Finn good night for me," Mr. Schenkel said.

But Finn was gone.

Brian had told him he was going home with his dad the way he'd told his dad he was going home with Finn. And he'd called his mom and told her he was a total idiot, he'd forgotten to tell her that with an afternoon game tomorrow, he and Finn were doing another sleepover at Comerica.

But only he was.

CHAPTER 20

He hadn't wanted to take the ride home with his dad because he didn't want to talk to him anymore. He didn't want to hear his dad say what he'd tried to say outside the clubhouse, how things were going to be different with them from now on.

Better.

Brian *knew* better than that. Things were never going to change between them, never going to get better, whether his dad was there or here. Not in a million years.

And he knew something else: He didn't want to come home and have his mom be waiting up for him, as she'd said she was going to be, and have to talk about his dad.

He just wanted to be alone.

Brian wanted the ballpark to make him feel the way he did the first time he'd slept over.

Maybe he wanted it to make him the way it had always made his dad feel, like it was all he needed, like it was the only place in the world he really wanted to be.

He waited a few minutes until he was sure it was safe to go back in the clubhouse, walked up the hallway and up the steps and through the door, found the blanket and pillows where he knew Mr. Schenkel left them in one of the closets, and laid them neatly on the couch he'd used the first night.

If anybody came in and found him, from security or from the grounds crew who'd hung around late, he would just say that his mom was late, that she was coming, and that he was just waiting inside.

He stayed inside the clubhouse a long time, not turning on the television, just sitting there, feeling like he wanted to pull the whole place over him. Finally he looked up at the clock. Almost two in the morning now. He still didn't feel like sleeping. He'd felt tired all day, exhausted sometimes, yet now he couldn't sleep. So he walked down to the dugout and then up onto the field, took a few steps up on the field the way he had the first time.

But tonight he didn't want to go stand at home plate or run around the bases.

Instead he stood on the dugout steps and turned around

and looked up into the stands, and for the first time he could no longer imagine himself and his dad sitting there together. Tonight he had no desire, none, to go up and sit with his own memories up in Section 135.

Instead, Brian looked to his left, to Section 130.

The seats in Section 130 were all he could see and all he cared about. He just saw his dad in there with the other scouts, looking as happy as if he were at his own birthday party.

It was why the ballpark didn't make things better for Brian tonight, why baseball couldn't make things better. Or fix things with his dad. He wasn't sure anything could.

He'd found out something tonight:

It didn't matter to his dad who was sitting with him at a ballgame.

And no matter how much Brian loved baseball, it was never going to make his father love him more.

CHAPTER 21

It had been two weeks since Brian's dad had left town, and the beginning of his last month on the job was coming up so fast he couldn't believe it.

The first-place Tigers were at home for a weekend series against the second-place Indians, and all three games were at night, including another Sunday nighter on ESPN. It meant that Brian could play both games of a two-game series, Saturday afternoon and Sunday afternoon, against Birmingham, always one of the best teams in their league.

But he would have been better off going to work early.

Both days.

The Sting won both games, no problem there. Just no

thanks to him. He was 0-for-3 on Saturday with a walk. The only time he put the ball in play on Saturday was a ground ball to second off the end of his bat. When he finally did squeeze a walk out of one of the Birmingham relievers his last time up, he felt like asking the home-plate ump for the ball as a souvenir.

Sunday was even worse: three more strikeouts, and a foul-out to third. At least his mom didn't try to give him any kind of pep talk on the ride to Comerica. He rode in the car in silence almost all of the way, not talking about the game at all, not opening up about it until he was changing into his batting-practice outfit in Equipment Room No. 3 with Finn.

"I'm thinking about quitting the team," he said.

"Sure you are."

"I mean it.

"Actually, you don't," Finn said. "I've known you only a few months, and I still know you well enough to know that's not you."

"*I'm* not me anymore when it comes to swinging a bat."

"Your problem, far as I can tell, is that you don't get *enough* swings."

"That's what my friend Kenny says."

"Clearly a genius," Finn said. "You just gotta take a chill pill."

Brian made a sound like he was in pain. "Please don't tell me I've just got to relax."

They continued dressing in silence, and as they were about to leave, Finn said, "Wait, I *am* a genius."

"Glad you think so."

"Dude, I mean it, hear me out: Why don't you use the batting cage *here*?"

"Oh, yeah. Right. Sick idea. I saw Curtis down there using it before. I'll just run down and tell him he's got to clear out for, wait, the *batboy*."

"I don't mean now," Finn said. "After the game."

"*Tonight's* game?"

"Why not? We'll work it out with Mr. S. and then I'll just tell my mom to come a half hour later."

"It doesn't matter when your mom comes, Mr. S. isn't going to go for this in like a million years."

"We won't know that until we ask," Finn said. "Right?"

"Dubious," Brian said. "Extremely dubious."

Finn grinned at him. "See that, Debbie Downer? You didn't tell me we *weren't* going to ask, now, did you?"

They waited until they were finished with their pregame chores before taking the walk to Mr. Schenkel's office as if walking to the principal's office. When they got there, he was behind his desk, reading glasses on the end of his nose, going over the pregame media notes the way he did every day.

He looked up now over his glasses and said, "You two look like somebody just stole home plate. And I don't mean because the pitcher didn't check the runner at third."

Brian and Finn both cleared their throats at the same time. The sound effect was funny enough in the office to get a laugh out of Mr. S.

"I know you guys have grown close," he said, "but this is ridiculous."

"We were just wondering . . . ," Brian said. "Actually, the truth is, *I* was wondering . . ."

"No," Finn said, "we both were, he was right the first time. . . ."

Brian said, "If it would be okay with you, I mean once everybody is gone, of course . . ."

Mr. S. smiled, nodded, like he understood what they were talking about.

"And if it's not against team rules," Brian said, "if nobody would get in trouble . . ."

Mr. Schenkel took off his glasses and said to Brian, "Son, it's a good thing you write a letter of application better than you talk."

Finn jumped in again, this time like he was trying to save Brian from drowning.

"The thing is," he said, talking fast, "Brian is in a terrible slump with his travel team, can't buy a hit, pretty much can't remember the last time he got one, and he doesn't get enough BP because of his job here, so basically we were wondering if after everybody clears out tonight, well, if we could use Iron Mike in the batting cage."

All in one breath.

"Let me get this straight," Mr. Schenkel said, looking at Brian again. "*You* want to take *my* pitching machine out for a spin?"

Brian cleared his throat again and said, "Pretty much. Yeah."

The Tigers hitters didn't use Iron Mike anymore. When they wanted to hit indoors, they generally just asked one of the coaches to pitch. Or they hit off a tee. Or worked with this gadget that had "ocular" in the name, one that fired tennis balls at them from close range to improve their hand-eye reaction time.

But when the Tigers had moved to Comerica from the old Tiger Stadium, Mr. S. couldn't bear leaving Iron Mike behind. The machine wasn't as old as the ballpark, was actually fairly new, but to him it was one more symbol of the team's past and he wasn't willing to leave it behind.

"My machine, our cage, your BP," Mr. S. said.

"Something like that," Brian said.

"You know this is something I'd have to clear with the manager?"

Now Brian was the one talking fast. "Mr. S., if it's a problem, if even asking would be some kind of problem for you . . ."

"Hush now and get back to work and later on I'll get back to you."

He found them in the dugout a half hour later. Brian tried to read his face, couldn't. "Well," Mr. S. said. "At least I tried."

"He said no?" Brian said.

"No."

"Knew it."

"Hush again," Mr. S. said. "No, what he *said* was, and I quote, 'I don't want to know about this.' End quote. Which is now my official position as well."

Brian said, "So I can do it?"

Mr. Schenkel walked away, saying, "Do what? I have no idea what you're talking about."

Brian wasn't kidding himself into thinking that a few minutes in the cage, or a lot of minutes in the cage, were going to fix a swing that was about as graceful lately as if he were swinging blindly at a piñata at a party.

And it wasn't like he was going to be standing in there at Comerica in a real game, against real pitching.

Still.

For a little while tonight, *he* was going to get some hacks where *they* did.

But when the game was over, and the Tigers had lost 2–1 to the Indians, Brian had a thought:

He was going to take some hacks with *what*?

As he and Finn were stacking the boxes of gum and sunflower seeds for the night, Brian said, "I don't have a bat. Unless you've noticed a bunch of aluminum bats lying around here."

"I got you," Finn said. "I mean, I *so* got you. Willie said you could use one of his, that only chopsticks are lighter than his bats."

"You *told* him?"

"Don't worry, he says he won't tell and he's totally cool with it. Said if he didn't have a date, he'd be your personal batting instructor."

Brian stayed in his uniform when the game was over, figuring if he was going to take batting practice at Comerica, he would at least be dressed for the part. When they had finished all of their chores except shining shoes—which Finn said he'd take care of that night while Brian was hitting—Finn helped him wheel what was officially called the M6 Iron Mike out of the closet and down into the cage.

Brian already knew how to operate it because Mr. Schenkel had shown him and Finn how the first time he'd shown them Iron Mike. They knew that its hopper could handle up to 600 balls, but Brian figured a lot fewer than that would do tonight. He grabbed two bags of beat-up batting practice balls and fed them into the machine.

Finally he was in the cage, setting the speed at something he figured he could handle at the start—75 mph. Then he ran back and forth between Iron Mike and where home plate was in the cage a couple of times, to make sure the height of the pitches was set right.

When he had everything the way he wanted, he stood in there with Willie Vazquez's bat and swung. He missed the first couple of pitches, but on the third pitch he connected, what would actually have been a nice shot up the middle in a real game, and he couldn't believe how loud the sound of the ball on a wooden bat was in the quiet underneath Comerica. The sound jarred him and he grew nervous all over again.

He started thinking about his swing, and suddenly felt exactly the way he had with the Sting for the last month: lost. He began pulling off the ball, dropping his back shoulder no matter how hard he tried not to.

Before long he had gone through the first hopper of balls and decided he wasn't going to waste his time much longer, he'd load Iron Mike up once more and then call it a night.

He always heard the Tigers' hitters talking about how they had to make themselves wait at the plate. Yeah, Brian thought now, still flailing away at air, I'm waiting all right.

Waiting to feel like a hitter again.

He was about halfway through the last batch of balls when he heard somebody's voice in the runway. All the players were gone, so it had to be Mr. S. or Finn, maybe Finn coming down to tell him his mom was here and it was time to go, wrap it up.

My pleasure, Brian thought. One more good swing, if I've got one in me, and then I'm gone. He watched the mechanical arm of Iron Mike come forward, watched the ball as if it were coming out of a pitcher's hand, loaded up for a big swing.

And dropped his stupid shoulder again.

If this were a game, it would have been a straight-up-in-the-air pop-up.

"What kind of swing is that?"

No, Brian thought, the minute he heard the voice.

No no *no.*

He thought of the old John McEnroe line: You can*not* be serious!

The voice belonged to Hank Bishop.

Not just the last guy in the world Brian wanted to see right now.

Hank was the last guy in the world he wanted to see *him.*

CHAPTER 22

The balls kept whizzing by Brian, one nearly clipping him before he realized he'd taken a step in Hank's direction and jumped back.

"You're . . . you're not supposed to be here," Brian said.

"Shouldn't that be my line?"

Brian said, "I thought everybody . . . all the players . . . were gone."

"Forgot my cell phone, then I heard somebody in here," Hank said, showing it to Brian. Now he nodded at Iron Mike. "What's your excuse?"

"My poor excuse for a swing."

"Calling that a swing is pretty generous, kid," he said, looking disgusted, like the batting cage was one more place where Brian came up short.

The hopper was empty by now. Brian thought, Just pick up the balls, wait for Finn to help you roll it back, and get out of here.

"Load it up and let me see it again," Hank said.

"I'm sorry?"

"You're here to hit," Hank said, snapping at him. "So let me see you hit."

Brian filled up one of the bags, ran up and loaded up the ball hopper. Hank was still on the other side of the netting. Brian ran back to the plate. When the first pitch came at him, he didn't even swing, he was too busy watching Hank instead of the ball.

"Don't watch *me*, you idiot! Watch the ball!"

Brian swung and missed.

Then again.

And again.

Finally he made contact. He went through pitch after pitch, missing a lot more than he hit. And then finally Iron Mike was still and the cage was silent.

"I'm done," Brian said, dropping the bat.

"No, you're not," Hank Bishop said. "Go load that sucker up again." He shook his head. "If I left you here like this, with *that* swing, it would be like leaving the scene of a crime."

Then, to Brian's amazement, he stepped inside the cage.

Brian had no way of knowing if Finn might be watching from somewhere, probably as shocked as Brian at what was going on. Or if Mr. Schenkel might be taking in the show.

But he didn't care. He didn't have *time* to care because he was too busy listening to everything his new batting coach had to say.

Even if Hank Bishop was acting as if somebody was *making* him do this.

The first thing he'd done was order Brian to slow down the amount of time between pitches, so balls wouldn't be flying past them while he was talking.

"Seriously?" he said to Brian. "Has anybody who actually knew what he was doing ever worked with you on hitting?"

"Some of my coaches."

Hank shook his head. "Coaches in what *sport*?"

"I mean, my coach during the regular season this year a little bit . . . But there's a lot of guys on the team, and he can't—"

"More information than I was looking for. What about your dad?"

"Sure," Brian said. "You know, the basics when I was first

starting in T-Ball. But he sort of lost interest in my baseball career when he realized I couldn't pitch."

"Don't take this the wrong way? But neither could he. At least not the way he seems to think he could."

Maybe there was a time when he would have defended his dad. Not now. He just took his stance with Willie's bat in his hands as he heard the balls in Iron Mike's hopper start to move.

Hank came around behind him and jerked the bat down, startling him.

"Carry your hands lower," Hank said. "You've developed this god-awful hitch when you drop them and it throws your timing completely off, not to mention your stride. The idea is to keep things level."

"Feels weird."

"Pity. Do it."

A pitch came in. Brian swung and made contact. Not great contact. But he hadn't swung through this one.

"Wait!" Hank said. "And that doesn't just mean with your hands. Keep your weight back, too. That way, when every-thing comes through, it all comes through together: hands, shoulders, hips, all the torque in your lower body." He put his hands on Brian's shoulders and turned them hard to-ward Iron Mike, nearly knocking him over. "Theoretically, anyway."

Hank was wearing jeans, a plain white T-shirt, plain white

Nike sneakers. Now he took the bat out of Brian's hands, stood in there himself, and showed him what he'd been trying to tell him. He seemed to hit the first ball he saw so hard Brian thought he could have split it in two.

The sound of the ball on Willie's bat was a lot different, a lot louder, than it had been for Brian.

Hank handed him the bat. "And stop moving your feet all around, you look like you're sliding around on ice," he said. "Anchor that back foot, and when you stride with your front don't act as if you're trying to jump out of the stupid box."

On the next pitch Brian didn't stride at all, doing a terrible impression of Hank's swing.

"What was *that*?"

"Tried to shorten my stride."

Hank shook his head. "I said anchor the *back* foot." Shaking his head again, he said, "Scrub."

But he didn't leave.

Before they were finished, he changed Brian's hands again, pulling them back more. Kept telling him not to squeeze the handle so tight, like he was trying to grind it into sawdust. He had Brian open his stance slightly, moving his front foot back and pointing it more toward where third base would have been, as a way—he said—of getting Brian to clear his hips.

And more than anything he kept telling him—*yelling* at him—to keep his head on the ball.

"You know where it started with Ted Williams?" Hank said. "His eyes. His focus on the ball. They used to say he could read the words on a record going around at 78 rpm's."

"Seventy-eight . . . huh?"

Hank rubbed his face hard with both hands. "Never mind," he said. "I *have* figured out *some*thing, though."

"What?"

"You are your old man's kid," he said. "Because you hit exactly like a pitcher." And for the first time that night, he smiled.

Brian didn't know how long they'd been in there together, or how many times he'd refilled the hopper. He kept expecting Hank to kick him out. But as he stayed longer, no matter how sarcastic he got every time Brian did something wrong, an amazing thing began to happen:

Brian started to get it.

Started to feel as if he knew what he was doing and could have sworn he saw his bat *on* the ball a few times even though he'd been told that was impossible.

Finally Hank said, "Ten more swings, and please try to make it look as if I didn't waste my time here." Then he jogged up to Iron Mike and told Brian he was dialing up the speed to 85 mph, Brian knowing that was as much heat as he was ever going to face with the Bloomfield Sting.

On the sixth pitch—Brian having told himself it was 3–2,

bases loaded, bottom of the ninth—he waited and exploded on the ball and hit this *sweet* line drive that banged hard off the protective padding in front of Iron Mike.

"Quit on that one," Hank said.

"Was going to."

"Just do it like that from now on and you'll be fine," Hank said, already reaching into the front pocket of his jeans for his cell. "If you're going to play this game, play it the right way."

When he heard that—do it the right way—it made Brian want to ask him the same question he always wanted to ask him, about the steroids. But he didn't. Not tonight. He wasn't going to do anything to screw up tonight.

He watched as Hank punched out a number on his phone, walked through an opening in the netting, and said into the phone, "Leaving now. Got held up."

He didn't say good night to Brian. He just walked up the runway toward the clubhouse stairs, Brian hearing his voice until he disappeared.

Brian collected the balls, stuffing them into the two bags. He looked up and saw Finn standing on the other side of the netting.

Finn said, "I saw."

"How much?"

"The last few minutes."

Kneeling there, Brian said, "Wow," feeling the smile on his face.

"Yeah—wow," Finn said. "Now we gotta roll, 'cause my mom's been out there waiting and I think she's getting ticked."

"You go," Brian said. "Tell her I'll be right out."

Finn grinned at him. "Wow," he said again, and left.

Brian ran the two bags of balls into No. 3, came back, and wheeled Iron Mike back in there, back into its storage closet. He thought he was finished, then remembered he'd left Willie's bat and went back to the cage for that.

He was about to slide it back into its slot when he stopped.

He took the bat with him into the middle of the empty room, took his stance in front of his locker. Hands back, just the way Hank had shown him. Stance open. Head facing more toward the pitcher. Or where a pitcher would have been.

Hearing everything Hank had told him tonight as if he'd already burned the whole thing for his iPod.

Made sure he had room and then took one more big cut.

Yeah, he thought, smiling.

Yeah.

CHAPTER 23

The Sting were in second place in their league as they headed into August. And as hard as it was for Brian to believe, they were starting to move up on the end of the regular season, the league playoffs and the state tournament, if they won the league and made the states.

The Tigers were in New York to play an interleague series against the Mets. This meant Brian would get to play all three games of the Sting's biggest weekend of the series so far:

Clarkson on Friday night.

The Birmingham Bulls, always their biggest rival because the towns were so close to each other, on Saturday afternoon.

Finally, a game against first-place Motor City on Sunday afternoon.

The Sting were tied with Birmingham in second place, both of them two games behind Motor City. Clarkson was in third place, just a game behind the Sting and the Bulls. Everybody was trying to move up, because only the top four teams in the North Oakland Baseball Federation made the playoffs. The semis would be played on a Thursday night in Royal Oak, the week after next. The finals would also be at Royal Oak this year, again under the lights, just two nights later.

Brian had checked the Tigers' schedule when he'd first gotten the job, knowing when his league season would end and the tournament would start. So he knew that the Tigers would be in Cleveland the weekend of the tournament, and he would have no conflict and no worries if the Sting finished in the top four.

Making the playoffs was still no sure thing. But for Brian and Kenny and Will Coben and Ryan Santoro and the rest of the guys on the team, these three weekend games were the beginning of all that, the beginning of their own stretch run. It all felt like the playoffs.

In the big leagues, they always talked about the "dog days of August." But if you were fourteen and knew school was a month away and you were staring the end of your baseball summer in the face, there was no such thing as dog days. Even if you were in a slump, the way Brian was.

Brian felt that the best part of the Sting season was starting right now. And thanks to that night with Hank, he'd finally come out of his slump. His second time up on Friday night he lined a clean single to left. His last time up he hit one right on the nose, even if the ball ended up in the third baseman's glove.

For the first time in a long time, he wasn't chasing bad pitches and actually felt as if he had some idea about what he was doing at the plate.

"Hank says that when you chase, you don't just develop bad habits," he said to Kenny on the bench before Saturday afternoon's game. "He said you also turn bad pitchers into *great* pitchers."

Kenny grinned. "Oh, is that what Hank said?"

Brian ducked his head, embarrassed, and was glad they were at the end of the bench and nobody else had heard him. "I make it sound like the two of us are tight, right?"

"Oh, yeah," Kenny said. "Like that's the way the two of you roll."

"It's not like that."

"Dude, you don't have to explain," Kenny said. "I'm just fired up that *you're* fired up about your brand again."

Brand. One of Kenny's favorite words.

"I don't *have* a brand," Brian said. "Just one clean hit in the books last night and one that should have been a hit. Now I'd like to get a couple more and support our excellent starting pitcher—you—against our hated rivals."

"You sound like one of those guys on television," Kenny said, lapsing into his deep announcer voice. "Fans, these two teams really don't like each other."

Brian smiled at that and turned to Kenny, putting out his fist. It *had* only been a couple of good swings the night before. But they had been enough for Coach Johnson to move him up to second in the batting order, right behind Kenny, who would be leading off for the first time all season.

When Brian had asked him why he'd juggled the order, Coach had shrugged. "Got a feeling," was all he said.

Kenny had said, "Sure it's not gas, Coach?"

But Kenny made Coach look like a genius when he doubled over the right fielder's head leading off the bottom of the first. The Bulls also had their ace going today, a kid named Johnny Hastings, who was small but had a big arm.

So there was Kenny on second, clapping his hands, telling Brian to bring him home.

Wait, he heard Hank telling him in the cage.

Wait.

He took a first-pitch fastball for a strike, then laid off the next one, another fastball, this one just high enough to be called a ball—the kind of sucker pitch he'd been missing all season.

Wait, he told himself again.

Johnny Hastings didn't take anything off the 1–1 pitch. But this one was right in the middle of the strike zone and Brian was on it. Not over-anxious. Not anxious at all, actually. He kept his weight back. Kept his hands still and his rear foot planted and his head back—doing these things without having to think about them—and hit the ball as hard as he had all season long. Top-handing it—one of Hank's favorite expressions—just enough, putting just enough topspin on it that it became a gapper instead of a routine fly to left-center. Neither the center fielder nor the left fielder could cut the ball off before it rolled all the way to the wall.

Brian was running hard out of the box, not needing a lesson in what to do in baseball when you got all of one.

He didn't even hesitate coming around second, didn't have to pick up Coach Johnson windmilling him toward third thinking triple the whole way. He could have gone into the bag standing up but decided to slide anyway because sometimes you just had to do that. You wanted dirt on your uniform after a swing like that.

1–0, Sting.

His mom was working today, so there was no reason for him to look up into the stands, nobody to share the moment with. And it was all right with Brian for a change. Nothing was going to take this feeling away, being out of breath, heart pounding, feeling pure satisfaction.

He looked over at Kenny, who'd slid into home plate even though he hadn't needed to slide either. Kenny was back up on his feet now, uniform full of dirt, standing next to the ump. Kenny wasn't about to show up Johnny Hastings or the Bulls, not after scoring the first run in the game. He just pointed at Brian, grinned, and nodded. Better than anybody on the Sting he knew what Brian had been going through and knew how much giving one a ride like this meant to him.

Brian nodded back. Ryan Santoro, batting third, singled Brian home on the first pitch, giving the Sting a quick 2–0 lead. When he got back to the bench, Kenny pounded him some fist and said, "You know what happens when you start swinging the bat like this, right?"

"Actually, I don't. What happens?"

"You don't stop."

"And you know this because of one swing?"

"Yeah, as a matter of fact I do," he said. "And it's not just one swing, you had the two last night."

"Good point."

"I try to keep up."

After that it was just one of those dream days. Brian doubled to right his next time up, going with the pitch and hitting it to the opposite field, knocking in two more runs in the process. Now the Sting were ahead, 5–2.

The Bulls came back later when Brendan DePonte dropped

a fly ball he should have been able to catch with his teeth and gave away two cheap runs. But Brian singled in another run in the sixth. Three-for-three. The Sting ahead 6–4 now. Kenny, whose pitch count was uncommonly high today even though he had nasty stuff, was back at shortstop by then when Kevin Mahoney had relieved him.

Kevin gave up an unearned run in the top of the seventh. Sting 6, Bulls 5.

Some ball still left to be played.

When Brian came up in the bottom of the eighth with bases loaded and two outs, it was still 6–5. Not the first inning now. Not a 0–0 game. This was a Big Moment. The best kind. This was the kind of chance, game on the line, he hadn't had in a long time. The Bulls were going with a pitcher Brian didn't recognize, a tall kid who looked skinny enough to slip between the keys on his laptop, who came out with hard stuff and a lot of motion. But he got wild after getting the first two outs of the inning, hitting Andrew Clark before walking Brendan and Kenny.

No need for Brian to go through his to-do list as he dug in. He was locked in today. The only thing he told himself as he set his hands was to keep his stupid head still.

Hank had said, "You keep your head on the ball and sometimes the whole thing's as easy as hitting a golf ball off a tee."

Sometimes Coach Johnson had you take a strike in a situation like this, especially against a pitcher gone wild. Not now. Not the way Brian was swinging the bat.

The tall kid came right after him, not wanting to fall behind with the bases loaded, throwing Brian a fastball in a spot Kenny liked to call the middle of Woodward Avenue.

Like it *was* on a tee.

Brian hit this one even harder than he'd hit the triple in the first.

But this one had some air under it.

There weren't many fields in Bloomfield that had an outfield fence. The field at Way Elementary did. And as he came out of the box, Brian thought he'd cleared it.

Thought he'd cleared the fences at last. His first-ever home run.

You didn't stop to watch, didn't pose, not if you respected the game and the other team. So Brian came out of the box as if he were trying to leg out an infield hit. But eyes tracking the ball the whole way. Begging the sucker to get out.

One time, he thought.

He was around first when the ball hit about a foot from the top of the left-field wall and came off it in one hard bounce, right into the glove of the Bulls' left fielder, who wheeled and threw to second—a perfect one-hop throw that held Brian to a bases-clearing, three-run, stand-up double.

Brian had known when he stepped to the plate— everybody on the team knew—that a home run would have given him the cycle. And nobody in their league had ever hit for the cycle, at least according to Kenny Griffin, who said it with such authority that he made everybody on the Sting bench believe him.

Now Brian had come as close as you could come.

He didn't look in at the bench. He just leaned over, hands on his knees, out of breath, and stared at the spot where the ball had hit.

So close.

Brian knew he hadn't gone up there swinging for the cycle. Not thinking about it that way. But he *had* been swinging for the fences. He sure had.

No matter what, you had to keep swinging for the fences.

CHAPTER 24

Now Hank Bishop was the one in a slump.

Lost in what Willie Vazquez liked to call a "deep, dark forest."

It happened that way in baseball.

This wasn't a slump in the North Oakland league. It was one everybody was talking about—in the newspapers and on the radio and during Tigers games on television. By the time the team came back from New York to open a ten-game, AL Central home stand—against the Royals, White Sox, and Twins—Hank was 2-for-his-last-30 and his batting average had dropped to .227.

He was still stuck on 499 home runs. For three weeks now,

stuck. Knowing that everyone in the ballpark was waiting for number 500. Everyone watching on TV. He would see the larger-than-life scoreboards in every stadium, shouting out the number with every at-bat. So now he was pressing, feeling the pressure, just wanting it to be over. And the more he pressed, the worse his swing grew. Now the sportswriters were starting to wonder if the only reason the Tigers hadn't released him was because he *was* that close to hitting number 500.

Getting there, getting to 500, had seemed like a sure thing when the Tigers first signed him. Now Hank Bishop wasn't even a sure thing to make it to the end of the regular season, forget about what might be his last best chance at making the World Series. Mitch Albom had written a column in the *Free Press* the day before, speculating about the Tigers possibly releasing Hank, hoping that didn't happen, saying that's not the way the story was supposed to end.

Brian knew that in the old days, before the steroids era, 500 home runs really was one of baseball's magic numbers, and used to make you a lock for the Hall of Fame. But things had changed now. It had started with Mark McGwire.

Even though McGwire had never tested positive for any baseball drug and never officially admitted to ever *taking* baseball drugs, everybody assumed that he had because of that appearance he'd made before Congress. That was the day he'd said, "I'm not here to talk about the past," and the whole world had taken that as a full confession. Since then he had come up for election to the Hall of Fame a bunch of times and had never even come close to getting in. Then Alex Rodriguez admitted he'd used drugs, baseball drugs, when *he* was with the Texas Rangers. It came out that Sammy Sosa had tested positive. Manny Ramirez got suspended for 50 games when he got to the Dodgers. On and on it went.

The first day back with the Tigers, Hank Bishop had said this:

"Guys, I'm not going to defend my life every single day till the season is over. I'll just say there are a lot of things in my life that I wish I could go back and do over. And a lot of things I'm sorry for. I'm sure a lot of players from this era feel the same way. But I can't go back and change things any more than baseball can. What happened happened. And again, I'm sorry. I'm just trying to move forward now with my life and my career and hope y'all will let me do that. Let my bat speak for me from now on."

Trouble was, Hank's bat had grown awfully silent.

Lately, he was lucky to get his name written into Davey's batting order a couple of days a week.

Maybe that was why at two o'clock in the afternoon of the first game of the Royals series Hank was out on the field, despite the fact that the temperature was trying hard to get to 100 degrees today, having Rudy Tavarez throw him early batting practice.

Brian was at Comerica early. He had gotten into his pre-game outfit, Mr. S. telling him shorts were allowed today, and decided to get a jump on his pregame chores. So he brought the towels up and stacked them neatly in the dug-out, brought the trays of gum and the bags of sunflower seeds, the rosin bags, rolled the bat cart up the runway and organized the bats in the rack, wanting to have all of that done before Finn arrived.

It was all part of Brian's plan.

Brian was sweating like crazy by the time he finished organizing the helmets, so he took a seat in the corner of the dugout and watched Hank work with Rudy. Hank had already sweated through his gray Tigers T-shirt with the sleeves cut off, his batting-practice cap so wet it looked as if he had taken a shower in it.

Every once in a while he would stop to towel off and take a quick swig of Gatorade from the bottle he'd tossed in the grass. Mostly he worked. One of the Tigers' young mid-dle relievers, Nick O'Meara, was shagging the balls in the outfield, throwing them back in. When Rudy and Hank would go through a bucket, they'd just start again. Hank hit some balls hard, even jacking one into the seats. But mostly he was pressing the way he had been in games for the past few weeks, even against a coach trying to groove pitches for him, a coach who wanted to get taken out of the yard.

Finally Rudy said, "You want to stop?"

"No."

"We could take a break, 'fore you pass out from the heat."

"No."

"Well, at least let's slow down the pace a little here. I'm about to pass out. Besides, it's no good to just keep beating balls into submission without thinking about what we're trying to do."

Brian felt as if he were eavesdropping, like somehow he shouldn't be listening to this, so he slid himself closer to the end of the bench, out of sight from home plate.

Hank, his voice loud in the empty park, said, "Rudy, *thinking* isn't my problem. That's one thing I can still do as well as I ever did. Maybe the only thing."

"Hank, my brother, you *got* to find a way to relax."

"Rudy, you don't understand!" Now Hank's voice was so loud it was as if it were coming out of the PA system. *"I'm running out of time here!"*

He was still in his stance, looking uncomfortable, Brian able to see how hard he was gripping the bat, the muscles in his forearms stretched so tightly they reminded Brian of a rubber band about to snap.

The way Hank Bishop had just snapped. It was as if he knew that now, had heard himself in Comerica.

"Few more," Hank said, lowering his voice.

He took a huge swing at the next pitch Rudy threw, what

Coach Johnson called a come-out-your-shoes swing, and popped the ball up behind second.

Amazing, Brian thought.

A guy with 499 home runs in the big leagues and he's as messed up as I was.

They finished up a few pitches later when Hank finally managed to hit one over the wall out to left.

"Let's stop on that one," he said, and Rudy looked relieved. Hank's blue Franklin batting gloves were dripping wet. He took them off, along with his cap, and he and Rudy sat down in the grass next to home plate. Rudy did most of the talking, occasionally standing up and taking his stance, pointing to his front shoulder, sitting back down.

They finally got up and Rudy told Hank he'd pick up the rest of the balls in the infield, that Hank should get out of the sun now. Hank started walking back toward the dugout. Brian had brought a bottle of Gatorade for himself, but now he came out of the shadows and up the steps and handed it to Hank.

"Thanks," he said, as if he was almost too worn out to say that.

"Hey," Brian said, "I never got to thank *you*."

"For what?"

"That night in the cage."

"Oh, yeah. Right."

Brian grabbed him a towel now from the stack behind the bench, handed it to him. Hank wiped himself off.

"Because, see, the thing is, the lesson worked," Brian said. "That's what I really wanted to thank you for. Got four hits right after that, nearly hit for the cycle, as a matter of fact."

"I'm sorry," Hank said. *"What?"*

"You gave me some pointers," Brian said, thinking he just hadn't heard, "and one of my next games, last time up, needing a home run for the cycle, the ball I hit just caught the top of the fence. . . ."

Hank brushed by him now, on his way down the steps, saying, "Not today, kid."

"I didn't mean to bother you," Brian said. "But I just wanted you to know. . . ."

Then Hank was as loud as he had been with Rudy Tavarez, slamming his bat into the bat rack so hard Brian was afraid he might break it.

"What part of *not today* aren't you getting?" he said. Then he disappeared down the runway.

CHAPTER 25

The next afternoon Brian and Willie Vazquez were in Equipment Room No. 3 after Brian had made his daily run to McDonald's.

The Tigers had won the night before, but Hank had sat on the bench, his average sitting with him at .218. Davey Schofield had just posted his lineup for tonight's game and Brian saw that Hank wouldn't be playing again, even though the Royals had a righty going.

"Ask you something?" Brian said to Willie.

Finn was helping out over on the visitors' side, one of the guys having called in sick. So it was just Brian and Willie, no other players having gotten in on today's order.

Willie smiled, his second Big Mac halfway to his mouth.

"You're my burger connection," Willie said. "Ask me anything."

Brian said, "Why do you think Hank did it?"

Willie put his burger down on the chair he had pulled up next to him and took a sip of Coke.

"Why he did what?" he said.

"You know what I mean," Brian said. "Why do you think he took the steroids?"

Willie took his time, wiping his hands with a napkin. Taking another sip of Coke. Smiling at Brian now, as if you couldn't wipe the smile off his face even if the subject was baseball drugs.

"Now, technically," Willie said, "the Bishop never actually admitted he *did* do them drugs."

Brian said, "But not only did Hank test positive, he tested positive after he knew he could get suspended for that. If the test was wrong, if it was one of those false positives, wouldn't he have said it was all a big mistake?"

Willie said, "You know what's amazing, little man? How much you got to talk about steroids in this game whether you did anything or not. I always thought that was the worst thing of all, how the innocent got thrown in there with the guilty. How everybody got turned into a suspect. Like it wasn't guilty or innocent after a while, like it was 'caught or not caught,' least in the eyes of the fans."

Brian said, "You ever try the stuff?"

Willie shook his head. "Nope."

"Think about it?"

"Everybody *thought* about it, little man. But I had a big brother got his life all messed up on other kinds of drugs, the worst kind, when I was little. Ended up in jail, even though where they should have sent him was to one of those rehab hospitals. Lordy, when I was growing up, my momma made me more afraid of drugs than of the devil. So I tried to do like the great Hammerin' Henry Aaron, the real all-time home run champ of the game of baseball."

"What?"

Willie smiled again and said, "Strongest thing I ever take is chewin' gum. And these burgers."

Brian said, "But there was a lot of it going on when you first came up."

"Course there was." Willie serious, as serious as Brian had ever seen him. Not smiling now. "I got eyes. I'd see guys who weighed 175 at the end of one season come back and be 225 and look like the Incredible Hulk. And this was even after the real testing kicked in. I'd just say to myself, Now there's a boy found a way to stay one step ahead of the testers. Or he just found something they got no test for. *Yet*."

"But Hank had it all going for him."

"Let me ask *you* something," Willie said. "Alex Rodriguez *didn't* have it all going for him? Barry Bonds?"

"That's my point—guys like that didn't need it!" Brian said, the force of his voice surprising him.

"See, that's the thing, though," Willie said. "They thought they did. Barry Bonds, he thought he had to do it to go past McGwire and Sammy Sosa. Then A-Rod, he must've looked at Bonds and said, I got to get past him someday, I better do what he was doing when he hit out 73 that one season. And all of them using that junk must've thought nobody would ever present them with no bill."

Willie picked up his Big Mac again, took a big bite. "I'm just speculating, mind you."

"You think he can ever be good again without it? Hank, I mean."

"You don't give up, do you?"

Brian shook his head. No.

Willie sighed. "I still think Hank Bishop's got it, somewhere inside him. Question is whether he's gonna find it before it's too late."

Willie got up now, thanked Brian for the food, and said, "Since we quoting all-time greats today, you know what Yogi Berra said one time, right?"

"What?"

"Yogi said it sure gets late early around here," Willie Vazquez said.

"I wish there was something I could do to help," Brian said.

Because he did want to help.

"You want to help that man even the way he treats you."

"Yeah," Brian said. "I do."

Willie was at the door. He came back, put his arm around Brian. "You a good man, little man."

Brian wondered if he had the courage to back up that claim, knowing what he now knew. Having seen what he was sure he had seen earlier today.

The Tigers won the last game of the Royals series, completing a sweep, 10–2. Davey had thrown Hank out there in the fifth inning, maybe thinking that on a night when everybody was hitting, it might be contagious. But even against a scrub reliever, Hank struck out twice—the second time looking.

Brian was worried that Hank might break another bat after that one, could see how red his face was after the home-plate ump rung him up on a close pitch for strike three. Even now, though, his season and maybe even his career slipping away, it was as if he knew you couldn't pitch a fit in a blow-out game like this, especially one your team was winning.

So he just walked back to the dugout, handed his bat to Brian, went to the far end of the bench, and sat there alone until the game was over. And when it was over, when all the other players and coaches and Davey Schofield were gone, he went back to work, alone this time, in the indoor batting cage.

Not facing Iron Mike the way Brian had.

Just beating one ball after another off a tee.

Finn was gone by then. Brian's mom was his ride home tonight and she had already texted him to say she'd be leaving work at the usual time and would meet him outside.

It was when Brian was on his way back from making one last sweep of the dugout that he heard the sounds from the cage and discovered it was Hank. So he hung back out of sight and watched while he went through a bucket of balls.

Brian couldn't help himself.

"I'll pick them up for you," he said in the sudden silence. "If you want."

"You don't give up, do you?" Hank said.

"Just doing my job," Brian said, squeezing out a smile. "Picking up balls is part of it, you know."

Brian came through the netting then. The two of them picked up balls together. When they were finished, Hank said, "You don't have to stay."

"I'm good."

"Yeah, just like me."

Hank readjusted his batting gloves, almost like he needed something to do. "Guy I used to play with said to me one time,

'When you're young and in a slump, it's just a slump,'" he said. "'But when you're old and in a slump, you're just old.'"

"You'll get to 500," Brian said.

"You think that's what this is about?" he said.

"Well, no," Brian said, almost like he felt his own words tripping him up. "I mean, yeah, I thought that was *part* of it."

"It was never about that," Hank said in a quiet voice. "Never."

He went back to driving balls off the tee, taking his time, checking his hands before every swing and setting them behind his right shoulder, setting them high, holding his follow-through sometimes. Brian stood there and felt as if he'd been watching this swing his whole life, as if this were some kind of old Hank Bishop highlight reel come to life.

Yet he knew better.

This swing was different.

Hank Bishop was the one carrying his hands too high, the one with the small hitch in his swing, throwing his timing all out of whack.

Brian was sure of it. He'd noticed it yesterday.

The question was, What was he going to do about it?

Hank valued Brian's opinion the way he would value a fly's.

"I'm swinging late even hitting off a stinking tee," Hank said now.

Okay, Brian thought, now or never. No guts, no glory.

He took a deep breath.

"You know, I've been noticing something, watching you."

Hank turned toward him, hands already cocked in his batting pose. Not looking at Brian in a mean way. Just slowly shaking his head. "Seriously? I've gotten advice from everybody, kid. And I mean *every*body. You should read my mail. Please don't you start, I'm begging you."

Brian put up his hands, making himself smile, feeling himself actually backing up into the netting as he did. "No," he said.

"No is right," Hank said. "No more talk."

"Got it."

"Excellent."

He took about twenty more swings, the swings becoming more and more fierce, his face looking more and more angry, sweat pouring off him at the end the way it had when he'd been taking his BP outside with Rudy.

Brian picked up the balls by himself this time. Hank had had enough for the night.

About fifteen minutes later they were coming out of the elevator together, walking across the lobby and into the cool night air. And the air was cool enough to make Brian think that his summer with the Tigers was beginning to come to an end.

He looked up and saw his mom standing near their car. "I was afraid I was going to have to come in after you," she said.

Then to Hank she said, "Sometimes I'm afraid I'm going to have to use the Jaws of Life to pry him loose from the Tigers."

"It wasn't Brian's fault tonight, Mrs. Dudley," Hank said. "It was mine."

"Liz," she said.

Hank grinned. "We've gone over this already, haven't we?"

"That we have."

"Your boy was helping me out tonight," Hank Bishop said. "Little late-night batting practice. Trying to break me out of this horrendous slump I'm in."

"And did he?" she said. "Help you out of it, I mean."

I could have, Brian thought. I just didn't get the chance.

Wimped out, totally.

"I'm not sure anyone can at this point."

"I can," Liz Dudley said.

"Excuse me?"

"I know exactly what you need, Mr. Bishop."

"Hank."

"*Hank*," she said. "What you need is a home-cooked meal away. Far away from baseball. Far, far away."

No way he says yes, Brian thought.

No way ever.

Please say yes.

"I couldn't," Hank said.

"Well, I insist," she said. "What about after Sunday afternoon's game?"

Brian stood there waiting, holding his breath, looking from his mom to Hank Bishop, still thinking, No way in this world.

"I accept," Hank said.

Way.

CHAPTER 26

Sunday afternoon. The Tigers had beaten the Twins 5–1. Hank even managed a clean single to right his last time up, Brian hoping that it might put him in a better mood for dinner, still worrying he might find some kind of last-minute excuse to beg out.

So in the clubhouse after the game Brian said to him, "My mom just wanted me to check with you, that you're still coming tonight."

Hank had already showered and changed by then. "Been a while since I've had a home-cooked meal cooked by anybody except me," he said. "So, yeah, kid, I'm still in."

Then he said he had to stop by his apartment on his way

to Bloomfield Hills and pick something up. Told him to tell his mom not to worry—he'd be there.

"You know," Finn said in his mom's car on the way to drop off Brian at home, "I've checked my own calendar and I'm actually free tonight."

"Dude," Brian said, "if I could, you know I would. But it's just supposed to be the three of us, Mom's orders."

Finn nodded. "I hear you. In our house you break Mom's orders and even one of those presidential pardons can't save you."

From the front seat Finn's mom said, "I always love it when you talk about me as if I'm not here."

When they dropped Brian off, Finn made him promise to send texts throughout the evening. Brian laughed and said he'd just set up his laptop in the middle of the table so they could video-chat between courses.

They were eating in the dining room tonight. Brian couldn't even remember the last time he and his mom had eaten in there. They always ate at the kitchen table when it was just the two of them.

And it had just been the two of them for a long time.

She had set the table with her best plates and silverware and glasses, even had two candles she said Brian could light when the time came. She had tossed a huge salad, was preparing to throw a couple of steaks on the grill, and had made one of Brian's favorite desserts, banana cream pie.

Liz Dudley was also wearing a new dress, a blue summer dress she had bought the day before.

"You look awesome, Mom," Brian said when she came downstairs in it.

She looked down. "It isn't too much?"

"Too much awesome?"

"I mean, does it look like I'm trying too hard?"

"To do what?" Brian said. He smiled at her.

She smiled back. "Shut up," she said, heading outside to check on the grill. But she looked happy, as happy and excited as he had seen her in a long time. Brian knew this was more than just dinner for her. It was a little weird, but he had to admit, he got it.

Hank showed up right on time, seven thirty on the nose. Brian and his mom were waiting on the front step as he came up the cobblestone walk with a bottle of wine in his hand.

He handed the wine to Liz Dudley and said, "A little contribution to this fine meal."

"Thank you," she said.

"You're welcome."

He was wearing a blazer and white button-down shirt and blue jeans and had even shaved, Brian noticed—something he never seemed to do at the ballpark. He somehow always seemed to be three days into growing a beard.

To Brian now he said, "Hey."

"Hey, Mr. Bishop."

"We're both off duty tonight," he said. "Let's make it Hank."

Brian said he was good with that and the three of them went inside. As they did, it occurred to him suddenly that this was actually *Hank Bishop* and that he was actually inside *his house*. It was as if Brian was getting the chance to meet him again for the first time. Thinking that if somebody had told him at the start of the summer that a night like this was going to happen—if somebody had *ever* told him that a night like this was going to happen—he would have laughed.

It was during dessert that his mom said, "I'm sorry things haven't been going as well for you as you must have hoped they would."

"Wow," he said. "Ain't that the truth?"

"I know you said everybody's off duty tonight," she said. "So we can drop this if you like and talk about something else."

Hank looked at Brian. "Your mom is a lot nicer than most sportswriters."

"Whoa," Brian said, "not so fast," and everybody laughed.

When the table was quiet again, Hank said, "Maybe my expectations for myself were overly high coming in. But I never thought I'd sink this low, to tell you the truth."

"Your batting average, you mean?" Liz Dudley said.

"I mean everything."

There was another silence at the dining room table now, feeling to Brian like the longest one of the night, until his mom said, "If I make up one more small pot of coffee, would you have some with me, Hank?"

"Love some."

Brian's mom said, "So why don't you two go into the living room while I clean up and get the coffee going."

"Please let me help," Hank said.

"Go," she said. "Both of you. If I continue to monopolize the conversation, I am going to hear it from my son when you leave."

Brian said, "We could sit in the den if you want, and watch some of *Sunday Night Baseball*."

"No, thank you," Hank said. "I've had enough baseball for one day."

So they sat in the living room, Hank on the couch, Brian across from him in one of the formal chairs he hardly ever sat in. They weren't in the ballpark world now. Just Brian's world.

"I didn't think my mom would start talking baseball," Brian said.

"It's fine."

"But you just said you were baseballed out today."

In a soft voice then, one Brian almost didn't recognize, Hank Bishop said, "I don't know if I can still do it."

Brian said, "Not true."

"Yeah, kid," Hank said, "I'm afraid it is."

"You'll come out of this," Brian said. "I know you will. You hit a great pitch today your last time up. The guy was sure he had you set up inside, and you stayed right with him anyway, went the other way."

"I guessed right."

"You've guessed right a lot in your life."

"Mostly when I was still the Bishop of Baseball."

"You still are."

From the kitchen they both heard Brian's mom call out, "Five minutes more, I promise. Try not to miss me too much."

"We're fine," Hank said.

"You can't give up now," Brian said. "You've come back from . . . You've come too far, is all I'm sayin'." Brian grinned. "And I know you say you don't care about the 500, but you're *right there*. And once you hit number 500, you'll probably hit six in a week. Isn't that the way it always happens when you bust out of a slump?"

Hank leaned forward, big hands on his knees. "I told you this before. It was never about 500. It wasn't even about playing in a World Series, as much as I'd love to do that."

"You will."

Brian looked past Hank, toward the door to the kitchen. Not wanting his mom to come back. Not yet.

Not right now.

Hank shook his head. "Why am I talking about this with you?"

Brian just came out with the truth then, as plainly as he could.

"Because I'm still the biggest fan you've got," he said.

"After everything I've done."

"Yeah," Brian said. "After everything you've done."

"Amazing," he said. "The way people stay with you."

"So if it isn't 500 home runs and it isn't the Series, then why *did* you come back?"

"Because I had something to prove."

Brian took a deep breath, let it out, said, "You mean to the people who said you were all about steroids."

Hank stared at Brian now, almost as if they both knew it was his turn to tell the truth.

"No," he said. "Believe it or not, it was never about them, either. I came back because I had to prove something to my*self*."

By the time his mom and Hank had finished with their coffee, it was nine thirty. Hank thanked Liz Dudley again, told her it was the nicest night he'd had all season.

Brian's mom said her goodbye in the living room, said she'd let Brian walk Hank out to his car.

"Maybe I could buy you dinner sometime?" Hank said.

You. Brian knew Hank wasn't including him, that Hank Bishop was asking his mom out on a date.

"I'd like that a lot," she said.

Brian and Hank walked outside.

"Well, kid, I'll see you at the ballpark." Then Hank opened his car door.

"Wait," Brian said.

Hank turned, hand still on the door handle, maybe hearing the urgency in Brian's voice.

"Wait?"

"There's something I need to tell you," Brian said. "Something I should have told you the other night in the cage. And if I don't tell you now . . ."

His words drifted away into the night air.

"Kid, we both know I'm not a patient guy. So tell me already."

"You're . . . You're not the same hitter," Brian said.

It actually made Hank Bishop laugh. "Now *there's* a bombshell," he said.

"No," Brian said. His face felt hot, as hot as his words had come out. "I tried to tell you the other night, but then you told me about all the dopey batting tips people have been giving you. So I chickened out."

Hank gently closed the car door, the two of them standing on the sidewalk. He shook his head, like he was trying to be patient. "Brian," he said. "*Son*. I know you know a lot about baseball. I get that. I do. But you're *not* a batting coach."

"You gotta hear me out," Brian said, his words echoing up and down the empty street. "I've been watching you my whole *life*. And I've felt like something was different for a while and then the other day I was sure of it. So when I got home, I watched my *Bishop of Baseball* video for like the nine-thousandth time. And . . . and then I knew what it was for sure. You're holding your hands too high and it's made your swing different."

It all came out of him like he'd ripped open a package of words and they were spilling all over the sidewalk between them.

"I haven't changed my swing in twenty years. My hands are where they've always been."

"No," Brian insisted, "they're not. Not by much, but maybe just enough to affect your timing."

"You're serious."

"As a toothache."

"Where's this video?" Hank said.

"In my room."

Hank's face turned serious. "Let's go have a look."

CHAPTER 27

They walked back through the front door, to the great surprise of Brian's mom. On their way up the stairs, before his mom could say anything, Brian just waved a hand and said, "I forgot to show Hank something."

Hank smiled at Liz Dudley and shrugged, as if telling her he was just along for the ride.

Brian thought briefly about how he was taking Hank Bishop into what had always been a little bit of a Hank Bishop shrine. But he couldn't worry about that. He wasn't going to let any embarrassment about hero worship stop him now that he'd come this far.

When they got to his room, Brian saw that he'd left his

laptop on, went into his closet, dragged out a box full of Hank Bishop stuff, grabbed the DVD.

"What else you got in there?" Hank said.

"A lot."

He was sitting on Brian's bed. Brian motioned for him to take the chair at his desk.

The video had come out after Hank's last MVP season, when he'd hit the forty-seven home runs. And in it, around all the interviews with Hank and his teammates and pitchers and opposing managers, there were all different angles of Hank Bishop's swing, from the third-base side, first base, from behind home plate, from the camera in center field.

Brian cued it to the night when Hank had hit three home runs at Yankee Stadium and barely missed a fourth, every one of them shot from the camera behind the Yankee dugout, on the first-base side.

Before the first home run, Brian froze the picture.

"Right there. Look how low your hands are," he said. "See that? You set them right there and they're, like, *locked* until you start your swing."

"Un-pause it," Hank said, staring at the screen.

Brian did.

The ball shot off Hank's bat and into the section of center field at the old Yankee Stadium known as The Black.

"Short stroke for a pretty long ball," he said. Nodding.

"Really short. And it's almost like I've got the bat sitting on my right hip."

Now came the second home run, down the left-field line. "You look totally relaxed," Brian said.

"In the zone." Hank nodded again. "I've been looking at a lot of old tape on me. Maybe I didn't go back far enough. I was more worried that my only problem was over-striding."

The third home run now. Same short stroke. Same result. Another one into The Black. Two in the same game.

"Back it up again," Hank said.

Brian did.

He wasn't sure how many times they watched those three home-run swings, and the one that Paul O'Neill of the Yankees pulled back over the right-field wall. But it was a lot.

"This is probably a silly question given that I have my own personal Hall of Fame in your closet, but do you have any film of this year's swing?"

Brian felt himself blush, but he knew this was no time to hold back. "I have a link on my desktop. Here." He clicked on the Tigers' logo and together they watched Hank strike out. Three times in a row.

"Well. I'll be . . ." was all Hank said. Then he said, "You got some balls and a bat?"

Brian said, "Sure, but . . ."

"Good," Hank said. "And we're gonna need a field with lights around here. You got one of those?"

"Few minutes away, in Royal Oak."

"Now here's the big question," Hank said. "Can you pitch?"

Brian laughed. *"No!"* before he said, "But I know somebody who can."

"Who?"

"My friend Kenny."

"One more thing," Hank said. "We're gonna need one of those screens to put in front of him."

"Done," Brian said, and then leaned down and tapped out Kenny's screen name, IM-ed him and told him he and Hank Bishop were on their way over to pick him up. They were going over to Royal Oak for some late-night batting practice.

"So we've got everything we need?" Hank said.

Brian put up his hand for a high five.

"Of course we do," he said. "What kind of batboy do you think I am?"

From the backseat of the town car, no traffic to speak of on the short ride to Royal Oak on a Sunday night, Kenny Griffin just kept staring at Hank Bishop.

"If it had been anybody but you," Kenny said to Brian, "I would have been sure I was getting punked."

Kenny shook his head, like trying to clear cobwebs away. "Me. Pitching BP. To Hank Bishop."

From the front seat Hank said, "Look at it this way: You'll probably get me out the way everybody else is these days." Hank laughed, but it didn't sound like a happy laugh. "This shouldn't take too long. I'll have both of you home before you know it."

Kenny Griffin said, "Mr. Bishop, all due respect? I've got nothing but time."

Hank Bishop had some bats in the trunk of his car, saying he always had a couple with him when he left the ballpark, even when he was a kid. Like they were security blankets. Or good-luck charms. Between those bats, the folding pitching screen that Kenny owned, and the two dozen baseballs he and Brian had collected between them, they had everything they needed. Kenny was wearing his spikes and his Sting cap, blue with a white *S*. Brian had skipped putting his own spikes on, was just wearing a pair of old Nikes, to go with the same outfit he'd worn at dinner.

The field at Royal Oak was deserted in the night, but the lights were on, the way they always stayed on for a while after the last softball game of the evening had been played. The field looked to Brian the way all empty ball fields did, even ones not maintained as well as this one was:

It looked tremendous.

As they walked toward the pitcher's mound, Kenny carrying the protective screen he would set up in front of him, Brian heard his friend say, "This is *mad* cool."

He stopped and looked at Brian. "Do you think he'll mind if we take some pictures on my cell when we're done?" He lowered his voice. "Me and him, I mean."

Brian said, "I'm sure it won't be a problem."

Kenny closed his eyes and said, "Mad, mad cool."

Brian got behind the plate, warmed up Kenny while Hank did some quick stretching exercises. He was still in his white shirt and jeans, Brian noticing that he at least had rubber-soled shoes on.

"Let's do this," Hank said.

He turned to Brian. "You ready to do a little running in the outfield?"

"Yeah, man," he said, and sprinted out to left-center, imagining that he had his iPod with him, that he was listening to his favorite baseball song, John Fogerty singing, "Centerfield."

Put me in, Coach, I'm ready to play.

It took Kenny a few throws to get the ball near home plate, Brian able to see from the outfield how nervous his bud was. Finally Kenny took a deep, exaggerated breath, nodded at Hank like he was really ready now. Brian watched as Hank nodded back, his white sleeves rolled up to the elbow, carefully setting his hands, even looking down at them before Kenny delivered the ball.

Kenny poured a fastball down the middle.

Hank missed it.

"Sorry," Kenny said.

Hank yelled back at him, "Never apologize for throwing a strike. Now throw me another one."

Kenny threw another fastball, down the middle again. And Hank Bishop, looking as still and sure as he used to, gave this one a ride, Brian knowing the ball was over his head almost as soon as he hit it.

Not only was it over his head as he turned and tried to chase, but he was pretty sure it was still rising.

From the pitcher's mound, Kenny yelled, "Incoming!"

As the ball landed on the other side of the fence with a loud thud, Brian heard the crack of the bat again, this sound louder than the one right before it. The ball cleared the left-field fence by even more height than the one before.

Not every ball Hank hit that night went as far, but most of them were pure moon shots. Brian didn't bother to chase them. He just stared in awe as ball after ball soared over his head, like fireworks exploding in the sky. It was like having his own private outfield seat at the All-Star Home Run Derby.

In between pitches, Brian could see Hank tilt his head down just enough to make sure his hands were set right. That's me, Brian thought, hitting coach to the stars.

When Kenny had thrown the last ball they'd brought

along, the three of them just stood where they were, the silence seeming to echo as loudly as the thunderous explosions of maple bat on hardballs that had filled the little ballpark.

Then Hank nodded, just once. "Thanks, guys," he said.

They were the two most unnecessary words in the English language for Brian and Kenny.

They dropped off Kenny at his front door, Kenny's mom and dad coming out to thank Hank for including Kenny in a baseball adventure like this.

"Your son's got quite an arm," Hank said to them.

Brian had never seen a smile like that on his best bud's face.

"I'm telling you," Brian said as they left Kenny's driveway. "This is going to be *awesome*. I can't wait until the next Tigers game."

Hank glanced around him and sighed. "You mean, if I can hit as well against big-league pitching as I can against a fourteen-year-old?"

"You felt like your old self tonight," Brian said. "Admit it."

"Yeah," Hank said. "For a few minutes, I did. Now I've just got to do it against someone throwing 95."

The car pulled up to Brian's house. Hank got out with him.

"Thank you again," Hank said.

"I really didn't do anything," Brian said.

"You did more than you know," Hank answered.

"What?"

"Gave me one more person I want to prove something to," Hank Bishop said. *"You."*

CHAPTER 28

So it had come to this:

If everything broke right, Brian was looking at the best week of the summer. Both his summers, actually. The one with the Tigers and the one with the Bloomfield Sting.

Both summers were ending fast now, like Brian was racing through the last few chapters of a really good book, having to slow himself down because he was so eager to get to the good parts.

Hank Bishop had four home games to hit his 500th home run before the Tigers went back on the road for three consecutive series, ending with three games in Seattle against the Mariners. More than anything, Brian wanted to be there when Hank made his own personal history. And at least proved some of what he wanted—needed?—to prove. If he could.

Hank's average had dipped all the way to .217, and with the Indians holding a one-game lead over the Tigers in the Central Division standings and the Twins having won eight of their last ten to climb just a game behind Detroit, there was talk that the Tigers couldn't wait much longer for Hank to rediscover his hitting stroke. The Detroit media was calling for the team to acquire a power bat, 500th home run or no.

It wasn't unrealistic to think the Tigers might release Hank Bishop by the end of this road trip if he didn't start hitting.

Part two of what Brian wanted to be his own dream week? The Sting had to win their semifinal game against Clarkson on Thursday night and then find a way to win the finals of the North Oakland Baseball Federation against the winner of the Motor City–Birmingham game.

If they could manage all that, then they would be on their way to the state tournament.

Yet the dream was off to a slow start. It's impossible to hit home runs while sitting on the bench, and that's exactly where Hank Bishop found himself the first three games against the Twins. He didn't get a single at-bat as the Twins took two of the first three games. Today they would play one of those rare weekday afternoon games before hitting the road—a "getaway" game, as it was known. Assuming the rain held off, that is. The skies around Comerica were dark and heavy.

Brian was talking about all this with his mom on their way to Comerica Monday afternoon.

"Doesn't the manager know about the batting tip you gave Hank?" his mom said. She was smiling. "The one that's going to change the course of civilization?"

"Funny, Mom. Good one. I should have gone right into Davey's office yesterday when I saw that he hadn't written Hank's name into the batting order yet again. Set him straight."

They were a few minutes from the ballpark, Brian thinking that there were only a handful of these rides left for them. And this one was even more special than usual because Liz Dudley was actually coming to the game.

And today, Brian had a feeling, Hank Bishop would finally be back in the lineup. The Twins were pitching a young right-hander named Kevin Cross, a kid with a 97-mile-an-hour heater. Even hitters completely on their game had difficulty catching up with this guy's fastball. Yet Brian knew that Davey wasn't about to deprive Hank, and all the local fans and media, one last chance at seeing number 500 hit at home.

So when Brian had called Mr. S. to see if his mom could buy a ticket to today's game, Mr. S. had told him, "Don't be ridiculous. I'll set her up with a great seat."

It was the first time in years that Brian's mom would be going to a big-league game. Brian hoped it would be a day neither of them would ever forget.

"Today's the day," Brian said to Finn as they went through their daily checklist of items in the dugout, making sure they hadn't forgotten anything. Even though by now they never forgot anything.

"For number 500 you mean?"

Brian nodded.

"Let me get this straight," Finn said. "*You're* calling *his* shot?"

"Something like that."

They went back to organizing then, checking things off one by one on Finn's list: gum, Gatorade, water, sunflower seeds, towels, bats, helmets, rosin bags, bat rings. Brian lined up the trays of gum, making sure sugarless was right behind where Davey Schofield sat, Davey sometimes going through half a tray of gum all by himself before the game was over. In the old days, Mr. Schenkel said, before the Tigers' manager got what Mr. S. called "religion" on living a healthier life, he used to chew tobacco. Now he chomped away, all game long, on sugarless gum.

"You're saying today's the day," Finn said, "even though your guy has gone, like, 2-for-August so far?"

"I *know* his stats," Brian said. "But what they don't tell you is that he's got his stroke back."

"And you know this . . . how?"

"Batting practice."

"We barely even watched batting practice today."

"I'm just sayin'."

Finn stared at him. "You've got that look."

"What look?"

Finn said, "What do you know that I don't?"

Brian grinned. "Dude, I wouldn't even know where to start."

One thing Brian knew was where his mom was sitting. Mr. S. had come through big time, getting her a seat behind home plate. Her view today would be almost as good as Brian's.

Brian knew Hank hitting his 500th home run would have been a much bigger deal once. If it had happened when it was supposed to, when he was younger. If he'd never used steroids and never been suspended. If some of the other steroid guys hadn't treated 500 home runs like some sort of speed bump to even bigger numbers.

But even with all that, it was still huge for Brian Dudley. And he knew it was huge for Hank, even if he kept saying that his comeback wasn't *about* the numbers.

Right before the first pitch, setting up his folding chair in its usual spot, Brian looked up into the seats behind the home-plate screen. There was his mom, wearing a Tigers cap she must have bought. She waved at him, smiling.

Brian smiled back and shook his head. His mom at a Tigers game. His mom *wanting* to be at a Tigers game. And now his mom gearing up.

Compared with the improbability of all that, Hank hitting one historic home run tonight actually seemed like cake.

Kevin Cross had won fourteen games already and was the clear front-runner to be Rookie of the Year in the American League. Not only did he throw pure gas, but he also had a hard sinker that most batters couldn't pick up until it was too late. That sinker was his strikeout pitch, and he'd made many All-Stars look foolish already, flailing off balance at a ball that usually hit the catcher's mitt only an inch above the dirt.

Eventually, hitters would see him enough—in person and on film—to figure him out. Yet for now, no one was happy to be facing him.

Brian saw Hank for only a minute in the clubhouse before the game, stopping by his locker just long enough to wish him luck.

"Hey, Coach," Hank said.

He put out his fist. Brian gently pounded it.

Brian said, "I'm just one more guy rooting for you today."

"Root hard," Hank said.

"I always have," Brian said.

Hank got his first shot at Kevin Cross in the bottom of the first inning, Willie on second and Curtis Keller on first with two outs.

Now, Brian thought. Pounce on this guy early, before he gets too comfortable on the mound.

Get it out of the way right stinking now.

The crowd wound up being a sellout, and as Hank stepped into the batter's box, there were cameras clicking everywhere, as if the thunderstorm that was threatening had already begun and lightning strikes were hitting Comerica.

Brian leaned forward in his chair and stared as Hank carefully set his hands. He cocked them on his right hip the way he had that night at Royal Oak, the way he did in the old video. Didn't even take a practice swing.

Just stood there, waiting, still as a statue.

Now.

Baseball announcers liked to say that if you were lucky, you got one pitch to hit every at-bat. Hank got his with the count 2–2. The scoreboard listed the speed of every pitch, and the one before it had been 95 miles an hour. The scoreboard said it was a "fastball" even though Brian knew it had been Kevin Cross' sinker. Impossible to hit.

Now Cross threw that pitch again, only without nearly enough sink on it this time. Hank was sitting on it, knowing what was coming.

And he missed it.

Didn't miss it entirely. He still got good wood on it. Yet he missed it by the amazingly small distance between the sweet spot and the end of the bat, the distance in baseball that changed a home run into a routine fly ball to left.

Hank ran the ball out, knowing it didn't have the legs to leave the park before the fans did, their sudden cheer bursting like a roll of thunder as the ball left Hank's bat. When the ball landed harmlessly in the glove of the Twins' left fielder and the bottom of the first was over, Hank ran back across the infield. Brian had already collected his bat. They met at the dugout steps.

Hank was the one who spoke.

"No worries, it wasn't the swing," he said to Brian in a quiet voice. "I was just a little over-anxious."

Brian laughed. "Well, I was a *lot* over-anxious."

Hank gently took the bat from him, went walking down the steps with it, Brian knowing he was on his way to the indoor cage.

His next turn at bat came in the bottom of the fourth. By this point Cross had settled in and was throwing bullets. Hank struck out swinging on three pitches—good morning, good afternoon, and good night.

The way the rookie was pitching, Hank would get only two more at-bats. The game was an old-fashioned pitching duel, the Twins up 1–0 through four innings, having scored their lone run on a home run in the top of the second. Both pitchers seemed to be growing stronger as the game went on.

The rain, meanwhile, was holding off despite the ever-looming threat. Time was running out with every pitch, and the fans could sense it.

Hank came up to bat again in the bottom of the sixth with two men out, the Tigers still trailing 1–0. Maybe Hank sensed time running out, too, because he swung at the first pitch. He got the barrel of the bat around late against Cross' fastball, grounding it weakly to the Twins' shortstop.

Inning over.

The Twins' second baseman led off the seventh with a single and advanced to second on a ground out to the right side of the infield. The way the Twins' rookie pitcher was throwing, Brian knew the Tigers couldn't allow another run.

Sure enough, out walked Davey Schofield, signaling to a lefty in the Tigers' bullpen. The Twins' cleanup hitter was due up next, and he had a habit of feasting on tired pitchers. Davey wanted a fresh arm to get the Tigers out of this inning.

The move worked. The next two batters, each free-swinging lefties, were retired on only five pitches.

Neither team advanced a runner beyond first base over the next two innings.

Now it was the bottom of the ninth inning. Hank, due up second, walked to the on-deck circle. The wind was blowing in hard now, holding up any ball hit to the outfield. The rain, just a threat before, was finally starting to fall. Yet no one, not even the umpires, wanted to halt this game where it was.

Brian sneaked a glance at Hank's face. He couldn't read Hank's expression, which was as serious as ever. Brian wondered what he was thinking.

The Tigers' cleanup hitter led off and watched as the first two pitches were delivered low. Two balls, no strikes. It was the first time since the fifth inning that Cross had fallen behind a hitter. Could he be tiring? Brian thought.

The next pitch, a 96-mile-per-hour fastball on the inside corner, answered that question. Strike one.

The pitch after looked pretty much the same, and the Tigers' hitter fouled it behind home plate. The count was 2–2.

Here comes the sinker, Brian thought. Lay off it.

The hitter did. Twice.

A walk.

That brought up Hank with a runner on first.

Would Davey let him hit? Or bring in a pinch hitter?

If Hank was wondering the same thing, he never showed it, just walked slowly to the batter's box, the wind and the rain coming at him just a little harder now.

The crowd rose as if on cue, the sudden ovation filling the

stadium, as if everyone wanted the Bishop of Baseball to know they still believed in him.

Brian looked up at his mom. She was standing like everyone else, cupping her hands to her mouth and shouting encouragement to Hank, words that were carried away with the wind and energy of the moment.

The Twins' closer had been warming up in the bullpen, but their manager left in the rookie to finish what he had started, the ultimate battle of youth versus experience.

Hank stepped in. Took a deep breath. Set his hands again. Stared out at Kevin Cross, oblivious to the flashbulbs going off yet again.

This was the best of baseball, Brian knew, whether a guy was trying to hit a milestone home run or not. This was the whole thing: pitcher against hitter. *This* pitcher's best stuff against whatever best Hank still had in him.

Neither one of them knowing how it was all going to come out.

Cross reared back and blew a high fastball right past Hank, the ball smacking the glove of the Twins' catcher before Hank had even finished his swing.

Now, Brian thought again. You can't let him get to his sinker. You've got to catch up with his fastball.

Yet Brian had just seen: Hank *couldn't* catch up with Cross' fastball. You couldn't will things to happen in sports, no matter how hard you tried, no matter what kind of magical powers you thought you had as a fan.

Brian put his head down and thought, Maybe next game.

If there *was* a next game for Hank Bishop.

He didn't keep his head down long. Good thing. If he had, he wouldn't have seen the picture-perfect swing Hank Bishop put on the 0–1 fastball from Kevin Cross.

Brian would have heard it, though.

And would have known.

Sometimes you could hear wrong. Sometimes you thought a guy had caught one and he hadn't. Sometimes the ball didn't have the legs or the elevation, or the wind would knock it down.

Not this time.

Not today.

This baby was on its way to dead center and on its way out of Comerica, leaving the big field here as easily as balls had left the field at Royal Oak last Sunday night.

Brian was standing now in front of his chair, the way Davey and the guys in the dugout were standing on the front step, watching the flight of the ball, watching Darby Kellogg, the Twins' center fielder, finally stop running and just watch as Hank Bishop's 500th cleared the wind and the rain and center-field wall.

By a ton.

A two-run walk-off home run that proved the Bishop of Baseball still had it.

Now the sound of Comerica was deafening and the lights this time were coming from the scoreboard as it kept flashing "500" over and over again. The sound system cranked out "Glory Days" from Bruce Springsteen so big and loud that Brian was sure they could hear Bruce and the band in Canada.

Hank made his way around the bases, carried by the music and the noise and number 500, and the Tigers were all up and out of the dugout, waiting for him at home plate as if he'd just hit a home run to win the World Series instead of an August afternoon game.

Brian quickly took his eyes off the field because somehow he knew his mom's were on him. Could feel them. He turned and there she was, smiling like she was the happiest kid in the ballpark. Like she was the kid who used to sit in Section 135 when Hank was young.

Hank reached home plate and seemed to be high-fiving the whole Tigers team at once. Springsteen was still singing. Comerica was crazier than ever, no one in the mood to leave just yet. Hank finally came out of the crowd of his teammates, a few feet from home plate, stopped and pointed to all corners of the ballpark.

While all that was going on, Brian sneaked around the

celebration, picked up Hank's maple bat in the grass on the Twins' side of Comerica, and ran back with it to his spot near the dugout.

That's where he was when Hank broke away from Willie Vazquez and Curtis Keller and Mike Parilli and Rudy Tavarez and walked over to him.

As if it were just the two of them.

Hank Bishop smiled now, as if the last part of the celebration was the most important of all, and he reached out with his fist.

Brian smiled back, and put out his own right hand. The two of them pounded fist in front of the whole place, Brian feeling as if he and Hank were sharing this moment in front of the entire baseball world.

"Thanks," Hank said.

"I didn't do anything," Brian said.

"You did a lot," Hank said. "You showed me how to love baseball again. And reminded me why I loved it in the first place."

Brian's answer was to hand him the bat.

"I guess this belongs to the Hall of Fame now," he said.

Hank Bishop shook his head, handed it back to him.

"No, kid," he said. "It belongs to you."

CHAPTER 29

The Sting won their semifinal game against Clarkson on Thursday night, the same night Brian came home to find out Hank had hit two more home runs, numbers 501 and 502, against the Indians in Cleveland, giving the Tigers a one-game lead over the Indians in the Central Division.

Brian had two solid hits against Clarkson. The second was a single with the bases loaded in the fifth as the Sting scored five and blew the game wide open and made Coach Johnson's pitching gamble—not starting Kenny Griffin—pay off.

Even though it was now a one-game season, he had started Brendan DePonte against Clarkson, wanting to save Kenny for the finals. Before the game Brian had been sitting with Coach the way he always did, the two of them watching the other team warm up, Coach explaining any changes he'd made in the batting order, just because he knew Brian cared. Because he knew Brian didn't just like to play the games, but wanted to coach them, too.

Without being asked, Coach Johnson had said, "Just so you know? I'm pitching Brendan because he's *supposed* to pitch the semis and Kenny is *supposed* to pitch the finals."

As if that explained everything.

"I'd do the same," Brian had said. "Clarkson's not as good as either Motor City or Birmingham, anyway."

Coach Johnson had nodded. "Brendan will win tonight and Kenny will win Saturday night and then we'll go to the states and figure out a way to win there."

"Sounds like a plan," Brian had said. "To get to Saturday night and *not* have the ball in Kenny Griffin's hand would be dumber than rocks."

Brendan gave up two runs in six innings before Will Coben finished up. Motor City beat Birmingham in the second semifinal. So the finals were set: the Sting versus the Hit Dogs, Saturday night at Royal Oak. Same place where Kenny had pitched to Hank the other night with Brian in the outfield running down balls.

Only this time it was all for real.

"Pitching to Hank was pretty great, don't get me wrong," Kenny said after they finished their warm-ups before the final as he and Brian sat in the grass behind their bench. "But this is better."

They were still at least twenty minutes from the first pitch. But the bleachers, on both sides of the field, were nearly full already.

"This is where you're supposed to be," Brian said. "*Zackly* where you're supposed to be, as Willie Vazquez would say."

"It's where *we're* supposed to be," Kenny said. "Dude, we are a team. Now more than ever."

"Hey, you two chatterboxes," they heard from behind them.

They both turned to see Kenny's dad leaning over the fence.

"You get good and warm?" Greg Griffin said.

Kenny grinned. "No, Dad, as a matter of fact I didn't," he said. "Decided to go out there in the biggest game of the year completely cold."

"Funny," his dad said. To Brian he said, "Is he this funny with you?"

"Never, Mr. Griffin," he said. "Unless you count the way he thinks he can beat me in the Home Run Derby."

"Now *that's* funny," Kenny said.

"Remember," his dad said, "don't try to do too much

too early. The only time you get into trouble is when you over-throw."

"Dad," Kenny said, "I got it. Swear."

Then Mr. Griffin gave his son a long look and pounded his heart twice and Kenny did the same. In that moment, even with a lot of green between them, it was as if they were completely connected, as if Mr. Griffin had reached all the way over to the bench and put his arm around his son.

It was funny. Brian was the one whose dad had played in the big leagues, played for a long time. But when it came to baseball nights like this, sometimes he felt as if he'd never had a dad at all.

In the first inning Kenny did what he'd promised his dad he wasn't going to do:

He over-threw as badly as he had all season.

By the time he'd stopped being wild high—or wild outside, or wild inside, or wild in the dirt—he'd walked two guys, hit another, and had given up three hits and the Sting were losing the big game 3–0 before they'd even come to the plate. Kenny got out of the inning without further damage only thanks to Brian running down a line drive in left-center that would have scored two more runs for Motor City, catching the ball for what was always the best reason in baseball:

Because he absolutely had to.

When he came running back toward the infield, having already tossed the ball back in, Kenny was waiting for him out behind second base, and the two of them pounded gloves.

"You kept us in the game and you might have kept *me* in the game," Kenny said.

"You're not going anywhere for another six or seven innings," Brian said. "And by the way? Those Hit Dogs have gotten the last run they're going to get off you tonight."

Problem was, the Sting couldn't get any runs off Adam Connolly, the Motor City starter, a right-hander with just as much stuff as Kenny had, and just as good a record during the regular season.

Brian was batting fifth tonight, behind Kenny in the three hole with Will Coben batting cleanup. He thought he'd gotten the Sting back in the game in the sixth inning, Kenny on third and Will on second with two outs, absolutely crushing a ball that he was sure was going over the third-base bag and down the line in left.

But somehow the Hit Dogs' third baseman did his impression of a Gold-Glove-winning major-leaguer. The kid timed the ball perfectly, dived full out to his right, and gloved the ball about two inches above the bag. It was the most amazing play Brian had seen an infielder—and that included Kenny—make in their league all season.

A hard out.

But still an out.

And still 3–0, Motor City.

Brian thought, My dream week cannot end like this. Cannot. Cannot end with the Sting getting *shut out* on a night when we have our best pitcher going and we're supposed to be playing our way into the states.

That's not the way *his* story was supposed to be written.

Brian found himself looking up into the bleachers behind him a lot as the game ground its way through the middle innings, looking for his mom more than he usually did, sometimes catching her eye, sometimes not. She was sitting between Mr. and Mrs. Griffin, Tigers cap back on her head, and when they would lock eyes, she would shoot him a fist of encouragement, or pound her heart the way Kenny's dad had done. Heart was one thing Brian had plenty of.

What he didn't have was a lot of time. Or a lot of outs to give.

The Sting finally got on the board in the bottom of the eighth when Ryan Santoro, their center fielder, tripled home two runs. But Andrew Clark, their catcher, couldn't get him home. The game stayed 3–2.

Kenny had exceeded his pitch count by then and couldn't talk Coach Johnson into leaving him in there to finish up the game. Instead he switched over to shortstop. The Motor City coach had also relieved Adam Connolly by then, replacing him in the eighth with the Hit Dogs' closer, Pete Torres, a right-hander who threw even harder than Adam did.

The Hit Dogs went down in order in the top of the ninth. Just like that, the whole season for the Sting had come down to this one half inning. One to tie, two to win.

Don't score at all and go home. Season over.

Coach Johnson told the team to gather around him in front of the bench. It was then that Brian heard the applause from behind him.

He turned around along with everybody else on the team, along with Coach Johnson, and saw all the people on the Bloomfield side standing. At first Brian just thought it was some kind of spontaneous show of support from the parents and grandparents and brothers and sisters and friends who had come to the finals, everybody trying to get the Sting amped for the bottom of the ninth, for last ups.

It wasn't. The fans weren't cheering for the Sting, at least not for the moment.

Weren't even looking at them.

Coach was standing now, looking toward the far end of the bleachers, saying, "You've got to be kidding me."

Then all of the Sting players were up, too, pointing the way the fans were.

Pointing at Hank Bishop as he came walking toward their bench.

CHAPTER 30

Brian walked around their bench over to where Hank was standing on the other side of the chain-link fence.

"You're supposed to be in Cleveland," Brian said. "In fact, I watched you *play* in Cleveland this afternoon."

Brian looked over his shoulder past Hank and up to where his mom was sitting with the Griffins and saw her laughing her head off as though this had to be a joke. It couldn't be real.

"One o'clock game," he said. "Went 3-for-4, couple of ribbies. Then got into my rental car. Punched in the address on my trusty GPS, here I am. You ever want to make the trip, it's two and a half hours by car, if you step on it."

"But how did you even know . . . ?"

"Your mom might have mentioned something," he said. "Besides, you guys were both at my big game. I thought I'd just return the favor. You up this inning?"

"Third."

"Set those hands," Hank said.

"Check."

Hank said, "And what else?"

"Wait," Brian said.

"There you go," Hank Bishop said, and then made his way up the bleachers. The fans started to applaud again, but when he got to where Liz Dudley and the Griffins were, he put a finger to his lips and pointed toward the field.

Coach Johnson got the team back around him.

"Hank Bishop did something the other night that maybe only he believed he could do," Coach said. "Now you guys go do something we've *all* believed we could do since the first day of practice."

Kenny was leading off the inning. He laced the first pitch he saw over first base, making second easily, so easily he thought about going to third. But he stopped himself because he knew it wasn't worth the chance, knew you never wanted to make the first out of the bottom of the ninth at third base. You have to give the hitters behind you a chance to do their job.

Tying run on second now.

Will Coben up next. He worked the count to 3–2, but then couldn't lay off a fastball up in his eyes, swinging right through it.

One on, one out for Brian.

He got up out of the on-deck circle, took a quick look at the stands, saw them all standing, saw Hank Bishop turning his mom's cap around on her head, like he was making it into a rally cap.

Hank standing there next to his mom, both of them here for him. Together.

Like it was strictly regulation.

When he came around the ump and the catcher, he took one more look up there and caught Hank's eye. Hank Bishop posed in his batting stance.

Setting his hands low. And still.

Brian nodded.

He looked out at Kenny now, who pounded his heart. Twice. Then Brian checked the infielders and saw the Motor City third baseman, the one who'd robbed him, basically sitting right on the line now, not wanting to let a ball by him for extra bases.

Brian dug his back foot in, anchoring it the way Hank had told him to that first night in the cage.

Set his hands.

Took strike one, a fastball down the middle from Pete Torres, a fastball so sweet he wanted to step out and bang his bat against his batting helmet, thinking he might have taken the best pitch he was going to see.

That the one good pitch for this at-bat might have just gone right past him.

Pete Torres came out of his stretch again, even as Kenny danced off second and tried to distract him. Brian kept his hands back.

And waited.

And when his hands came through, when his bat fired through the zone and he came in behind his own short stride and caught Pete Torres' fastball on the sweet spot, he knew.

He knew the way he'd known with Hank's 500th. Knew that he had gotten all of it. Not because of the sound of the ball on the bat this time.

Knew because this time he was the guy who'd hit it.

Greatest feeling in this world.

Brian came out of the box running, running for his life. But he kept his eyes on the flight of the ball as it headed high and hard toward left field, high up there against the lights of Royal Oak, up there against the baseball night.

Like one of Hank's.

Brian was still running hard when he got to the bag at first, taking it in stride on the inside corner.

And he never slowed down.

Even after the ball had cleared the outfield fence.

The Hit Dogs, almost in shock, were already walking off the field, heads held low. The Sting players? They'd already started the party at home plate.

Brian couldn't wait to get there.

He rounded third and tossed away his batting helmet the way guys in the big leagues did in moments like this. Then his teammates were giving him just enough room to jump on home plate with both feet.

Kenny was on him, pounding on his back, yelling, "Not bat*boy*, dude! Bat*man*! Because you are *totally* the man!"

Finally Brian broke clear from Kenny, and Will, and Ryan, and even Coach Johnson. He hopped over the bench and walked over to the fence where his mom and Hank Bishop were waiting for him.

His mom's rally cap still turned around on her head. She was beaming.

Then his mom's arms were around him and she was trying to say something but couldn't. The words came out as a laugh or a cry.

Or both.

Then he broke free from his mom and it was just him and Hank. Hank put out his fist, just the way he had after his own home run at Comerica the other night.

Brian reached out his fist, but instead of bumping him one, Hank reached out both arms and lifted Brian straight up, as if trying to raise him all the way up to the top of the night. Brian felt as if he had cleared the fence all over again.

"Told you to wait," Hank said.

Yeah, Brian thought, I waited for this, all right.

Waited my whole life.

Turn the page for a preview of **Mike Lupica**'s

HERO

THERE were four thugs, total gangsters, in front of the house with their rifles and their night-vision goggles. Four more in back. No telling how many more inside.

So figure a dozen hard guys at least, protecting one of the worst guys in the world.

Not one of them having a clue about how much trouble they were really in, how badly I had them outnumbered.

Hired guns, in any country, never worried me. The Bads? They were the real enemy, worse than any terrorists, even if I was one of the few people alive who knew they existed.

Even my boss, the president of the United States,

didn't know what we were really up against, how much he really needed me.

When he talked about our country fighting an "unseen" threat, he didn't know how true that really was.

When my son, Zach, was little, I used to tell him these fantastic bedtime stories about the Bads, and he thought I was making them up. I wasn't.

The snow was falling hard now, bringing night along with it. Not good. Definitely not good. I didn't need a blizzard tonight, not if I wanted to get the plane in the air once I got back to the small terminal near the airport in Zagreb. Which was only going to happen if I could get past the guards, get inside, and then back out with the guy I'd come all this way for. It meant things going the way they were supposed to, which didn't always happen in my line of work.

My official line of work? That would be special adviser to the president. A title that meant nothing on nights like this. On assignments like this. The real job description was fixing things, things that other people couldn't, saving people who needed saving, capturing people who needed to be stopped. Dispensing my own brand of justice.

Sometimes I had help, people watching my back.

Not tonight. Tonight I was on my own. Not even the

president knew I was here. Sometimes you have to play by your own rules.

On this remote hill in northern Bosnia, near where the concentration camps had been discovered a few years before, I had managed to finally locate a Serb war criminal and part-time terrorist named Vladimir Radovic. He was known to governments around the world and decent people everywhere as Vlad the Bad because of all the innocent people he'd slaughtered when he was in power, before he was on the run.

To me, he was known by a code name, which I thought fit him much better:

The Rat.

I was here to catch the Rat.

Me, Tom Harriman. About to blow past the guns and inside a cabin that had been turned into an armed fortress.

Almost time now. I didn't just feel the darkness all around me, as if night had fallen out of the sky all at once. I could feel another darkness coming up inside me, the way it always did in moments like this, when something was about to happen. When I didn't have to keep my own bad self under control. When I could be one of the good guys but not have to behave like one.

The me that still scares me.

Time to go in and tell the Rat his ride was here.

I should have been cold, as long as I'd been wait-ing outside. And I knew I should be worried about what might go wrong. Only I wasn't. Cold or worried, take your pick.

As I moved along the front of the tree line, seeing the smoke coming out of the chimney, seeing both levels of the house lit up, I did wonder if it had been too easy finding him. Wondered if the Bads had wanted me to find him, as a way of drawing me here, making me vulnerable.

But that was always part of the fun of it, wasn't it? The finding out.

Someday when Zach is ready, when it is Zach's time and not mine, I will have to tell him the truth about the Bads and about me, tell my kid that the most fantastic story of all was me.

But for now it was time to be the unknown hero again, with the jeep waiting for me on the access road, over on the other side of the woods, with the jet waiting a few miles away in Zagreb. This wasn't the Tom Harriman who testified in front of Congress and briefed the intel-ligence agencies.

This was the Tom Harriman who did whatever it took to get the job done.

I began to move toward the left side of the house, my

boots not making a sound, even on the frozen snow. One of my many talents, gliding like I was riding an invisible wave.

The front four men were fanned out about fifty yards from the cabin, carrying their rifles like they were looking for any excuse to use them. They didn't know what I knew, that even if they did get to use them, the guns wouldn't do them much good.

And just like that I changed the plan, called an audible on myself, came walking out of the woods, in plain sight, talking to them in their native language.

"I'm lost," I said. "Can you help me out?"

Every gun turned toward me as the guards shouted at me to stop. But I just kept smiling, moving toward them, asking how to find my way back to the main road. I was such a stupid, they probably never met such a stupid in their lives.

The guy in charge just shook his head, turned and said something I couldn't hear, and they laughed, all of them dropping their guns at the same time, like a fighter dropping his hands.

I was on them before they knew it.

It was as if I'd covered the ground between us in one step. Another of my talents. Michael Jordan or LeBron never had a first step like this.

I put all four of them down before any of them could

get his gun back up. Wondered if they could hear the roar inside my head, the one I always heard. It was never adrenaline in times like this, it was something more, something I'd never been able to understand. Or control very well once the bell rang. Most people only see it happen in action movies, one against four, one guy using only his hands and feet for spins and kicks and jumps. Only this was no movie.

It was over quickly, the four of them laid out in the snow, arms splayed like snow angels. Done like dinner, as Zach would say.

It was then that I heard the crackle of the walkie-talkie from inside one of the guards' parkas. Heard a voice full of static, asking Toni why he wouldn't respond, that if he didn't respond right now, he was going to come looking for him.

I didn't know whether the voice was coming from behind the house, one of the four back there that I'd seen earlier, or from someone inside with the Rat.

Someone on the roof trained a huge searchlight on the front yard, making night as bright as day. The first shot was fired then, from somewhere off to my left. Then another. I ducked and rolled and went in a low crouch in the direction of the front door. They were probably wondering how I could still be moving like this, how they'd possibly missed me from close range.

I didn't have time to tell them they probably hadn't missed, that if they were going to put me down, they simply needed bigger guns.

They weren't putting me down and they weren't stopping me. I'd come too far to get the Rat, to take him to the people waiting for him in London, the ones who wanted to either hang him or put him away for the next ten thousand years.

I made it to the porch, the gunfire still crackling all around me.

First floor or second?

He was on the second floor. Don't ask me how I knew; I just did. Call it a sixth sense. So instead of crashing through the door, I jumped up to the second-floor landing.

Don't ask about making a jump like that. You either can or you can't.

I smashed the window and burst through. There he was, the fat slob, trying to make it to the door, turning to fire a shot with the gun in his right hand. But I was across the room before he could do anything, slapping the gun out of his hand, putting my hand behind his neck, finding the spot, putting him out.

I dragged him the rest of the way through the doorway, the two of us in the second-floor hallway. Here came two more of his guys, coming up the stairs with their guns raised but afraid to take the shot because I had pulled the Rat up in front of me, like one of those Kevlar vests you see on the cop shows. I wondered if the vests ever smelled as bad as he did.

It was the stink guys got on them when they were caught.

"Boys," I said to the guys on the stairs, "I'd love to stay and chat, but we've got a plane to catch. And I don't have to tell you what security is like at the airport these days."

"You're not going anywhere," the first one said.

"Well, yeah, actually I am," I said, and kicked him and his friend down the stairs. Then I was over them, flying toward the front door.

I had the Rat under my arm now. I'd played lacrosse in high school, had heard a story once about Jim Brown, who ended up becoming the greatest running back in pro-football history. Brown had been a lacrosse star himself in high school and later at Syracuse. He was so much bigger, stronger and faster than everyone else that he'd just pin his stick and the ball to his body, run down the field and score, again and again.

They'd had to change the rules so guys like him couldn't do that.

I pinned the Rat to me like that now, backing away from the house as more guys with guns appeared from every angle, all of them afraid to shoot because they might put one in the boss.

I thought about dropping him in the snow so I could go back and finish them all off, because when I got going like this, sometimes I couldn't stop myself.

But we really did have a plane to catch.

So I turned and ran into the woods, not worrying about the hidden trees or branches. I could see in the dark, even without those fancy night-vision goggles the Rat's boys had been wearing. Even with the hard snow pelting my face.

When I got to the other side of the woods, I looked down to the lights of the jeep, making sure that no one was waiting for me there.

It was just when you thought the hard part was over that the real danger began.

Nothing.

I threw the Rat in the backseat and peeled away, hearing the sound of cars starting up behind me. I tore off down the road toward Zagreb, taking the first turn like it was NASCAR.

My ride out of here, a Hawker 4000, was waiting on the runway, which was already covered in snow. I had told the kid who helped run the little terminal for his father that I worked for his president. I didn't tell him why I was here, just told him enough to pull him into tonight's action movie, like the two of us were playing Bond or Bourne.

I'd overpaid the kid by a lot for fuel and maintenance and told him what time I thought I'd be back and told him to have the wings de-iced. If not, the whole mission was a waste of time. Doomed to fail.

His eyes grew wide as plates when he counted the money. Then he nodded and promised me he'd do whatever I needed him to do. I told him that when the plane was in the air to take the money and the jeep he'd loaned me and keep driving until daylight because if he didn't, the guys I'd gone after would be going after him.

I saw two sets of headlights now. They looked to be a couple of minutes behind me, maybe less.

I pulled the jeep up to the plane, untied the Rat, dragged him out of the backseat.

"Him?" the kid said. "It was him you were after?" He crossed himself. Twice.

"Yeah," I said.

"He killed two of my uncles," the kid said. "In the war. Can't you just kill him here and let me watch?"

"Not my brand," I said. "Sorry."

Brand.

Another of Zach's expressions.

The Rat started to wake up. Must be losing my touch, I thought. Usually the claw was good for a few hours.

This time I just slapped him hard, twice, and back out he went.

Headlights from the first jeep appeared at the far end of the runway as I got behind the controls and started taxiing away from them. Soon enough the other jeep came barreling behind.

It was then, in the lights of the Hawker, that I saw a figure walking onto the runway. A man. He wasn't trying to stop me, wasn't carrying a weapon. Wasn't doing anything except standing in the lights, like all he wanted was for me to see him, hair as white as the falling snow showing underneath the old cap he wore down low over his eyes.

What are you doing here? I wondered.

You're supposed to be on the other side of the world.

Not here.

I didn't have time to find out. The plane was already bumping down the runway, shimmying on the ice and snow. And we were airborne, the Rat and me, through the first level of clouds.

Gone.

I tried to focus on flying the plane, getting above the weather, flying until I had to refuel, as I knew I'd have to, between here and London.

But in my mind I kept seeing him on the runway, just standing there.

And that was the problem.

It was never what you thought, never who you thought.

I wanted to feel the rush you felt after you'd won, that feeling the great guys in sports told you they never got tired of. I should have felt great, really, bringing down the Rat, delivering him to people who'd been chasing him a lot longer than I had.

So why did I feel as if I were the one being chased? Even up here, all alone in the night sky?

Catch the Action!

Don't miss any of **Mike Lupica**'s baseball stories!

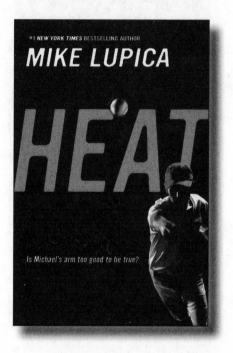

HEAT

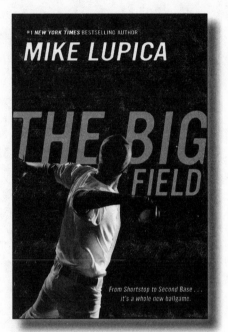

THE BIG FIELD